PRISONER 88

Leah Pileggi

Charlesbridge

To Kerrily and Angie D. and Shel

First paperback edition © 2019
Text copyright © 2013 by Leah Pileggi
Cover illustrations copyright © 2013 by Daniel Miyares
All rights reserved, including the right of reproduction in whole or in part in any form.
Charlesbridge and colophon are registered trademarks of Charlesbridge Publishing, Inc.

Published by Charlesbridge
85 Main Street
Watertown, MA 02472
(617) 926-0329
www.charlesbridge.com

Library of Congress Cataloging-in-Publication Data
Pileggi, Leah.
    Prisoner 88 / Leah Pileggi.
        p. cm.
    A fictional story based on a real incident as reported in a newspaper in Idaho
Territory in 1885.
    Summary: In 1885, ten-year-old Jake is sent to prison for killing a man who
threatened his father, and struggles to survive the harsh realities of prison life in the
Idaho Territory.
    ISBN 978-1-58089-560-6 (reinforced for library use)
    ISBN 978-1-58089-561-3 (softcover)
    ISBN 978-1-60734-534-3 (ebook)
    ISBN 978-1-60734-611-1 (ebook pdf)
1. Prisoners—Idaho Territory—Juvenile fiction. 2. Prisons—Idaho Territory—
Juvenile fiction. 3. Idaho Territory—History—19th century—Juvenile fiction. [1.
Prisoners—Idaho Territory—Fiction. 2. Prisons—Idaho Territory—Fiction. 3. Idaho
Territory—History—19th century—Fiction.] I. Title. II. Title: Prisoner Eighty-eight.

PZ7.P62849Pri 2013
813.6—dc23   2012024443

Printed in the United States of America
(hc) 10 9 8 7 6 5 4 3
(sc) 10 9 8 7 6 5 4 3 2 1

Display type set in Wausau by Yellow Design Studio
Text type set in Adobe Caslon Pro
Letter type set in P22 Monet Regular
Printed by Worzalla Publishing Company in Stevens Point, Wisconsin, USA
Production supervision by Brian G. Walker
Designed by Whitney Leader-Picone

ONE

May 31, 1885 – The Idaho Territory

Back before I shot Mr. Bennett, most every day was 'bout the same. Do what Pa said, work when I had to, eat when I could, sleep somewheres, start again when the sun come up. But after I got arrested, I didn't have Pa to listen to no more. He wasn't going to prison. Just me. Being that I was already ten and some, I figured I could pretty much take care of myself.

* * *

I hadn't never been on a train before. I stretched my neck tall to see out that train window. What I really wanted was to get on my knees and look out on the whole big world going by. But it was hard to move around wearing them big old rusty handcuffs, and one of the guards woulda smacked me. Alls I could see anyways was black smoke blowing back from that loud coal engine.

There was four of us criminals. Me and two old guys and one Chinaman. The Chinaman wore black pants, a black shirt, and a long tail braid down his back. The old guy with the beard wore a white shirt, jacket, and tie, but the ugly old guy weren't wearing much more than rags.

We didn't say nothing on that train ride 'cause we woulda got smacked for that, too. Right at the start the tall guard with the long mustache said, "Set down and shut up," and I wasn't taking no chances 'cause I believed him and his rifle. The other guard, the fat one with the red face, him and his Winchester didn't say not one word the whole way.

We got off the train in Boise, me and them three other men and them two guards. People stared at us shuffling along, our chains clanking and us looking all tough and mean.

Some train men lifted our belongings on top of a stage-coach. The beard man and the Chinaman had trunks. Not the ugly man and not me. I just had a old canvas bag, and he didn't have nothing. The red-face guard set inside, right between me and the window. The mustache guard set up front with the driver. I hadn't never been in a stage before either. Even with the windows open, it was rough riding and hot and smelly like to choke us all. I couldn't see nothing but the nasty rotten teeth on the ugly man setting across from me.

When the stage stopped, Mustache and Red Face pulled us out. We was all met by a couple more guards, both holding rifles in their two hands. We was facing a big old round-top wood gate set in a high white stone wall. On one side of the gate, that stone wall kept going. But on the other side, the stones met up tight with a high wood fence. One of them new guards, a young guy with a bunch of orange hair, seen me looking.

"The whole fence used to be wood," he said. "They're bringing in stone to finish it out."

I looked out beyond the wood section. Patches of scrub grass led up to the top of a steep hill where a cross pointed to the sky. I turned in a slow circle. Hills rolled up around us on most sides, like we was stew dregs in the bottom of a giant bowl.

The Mustache unlocked the gate. "Move it," he said. The guards pushed us through and locked the gate behind us.

We was led across a stretch of dirt toward a stone building. Bars covered the windows, and a long wire run from one of them windows across to what I figured out was the cellblock. We four men and four guards moved all clumped together into the building and down a hallway, and then we packed tight near the doorway of some special room. I knew it was special 'cause after our footsteps stopped making noise, it was so quiet I could hear my own heart beating in my ears.

A voice boomed, "Welcome to the Idaho Penitentiary, gentlemen."

Made me jump. Some hand come down on my shoulder

to keep me in place. I couldn't see who was talking 'cause I was tight up against the Chinaman's black shirt.

"I am Mr. Norton, assistant warden," said the big voice. "The door behind me leads to Warden Johnson's office. It's up to me to see to it that you do not end up in there during your incarceration." He grunted. "You will answer a list of questions for me before you're taken away. Otherwise, you will not talk, you will not move, you will not make a sound." I heard a *thump* and then papers flapping, like a big book flopped open. Then he barked, "You."

The first man shuffled on into the room.

"Prisoner number 85. Name?"

"Albert Meecham."

Sounded like he had a old dried-up frog in his throat. Had to be the ugly man.

"Age?"

I sorta drifted off about then, being kinda tired from the trip. I didn't listen again 'til Mr. Norton shouted, "Speak up, Mr. Meecham."

"Murder in the first degree" is what he said.

Then Mr. Norton's voice got kinda quiet and real deep. "Those handcuffs and Leininger shackles will become your close friends, Mr. Meecham. When you are out of your cell—if you are out of your cell—they will be with you every second."

Mr. Meecham didn't have nothing to say to that.

Mr. Norton kept on talking. "If at any time the warden or I feel that you are a threat to the guards or to the other inmates, you will be placed in the Hole. That's solitary confinement, sir."

I heard Mr. Norton cough up a wad of spit and let it go into some kinda container. Then he went right on talking. "The Hole's an unpleasant place to pass the time, Mr. Meecham. Do you understand?"

I heard, "Yeah."

"What did you say?"

Mr. Meecham's gravelly voice growled, "Yes, sir."

There was some scuffling, and then here come the ugly man with two guards holding him under his armpits. He grinned at me with them dead teeth as they took him out. Last thing I seen was his boot toes dragging behind him.

"Next," said Mr. Norton.

I could hear the beard man's arm irons clanking as he stepped ahead.

"Prisoner number 86," said Mr. Norton. "Name?"

"Joshua Nance."

"Age?"

"Sixty-two."

"Height?"

I heard some boots moving around, and one of them guards said, "He's round about six feet."

"Skin color?"

"Well, sir, if I could remove the travel dirt from my face and neck, you'd see that I'm a white man."

Mr. Norton said, "Did I ask for a story, Mr. Nance?"

"No, sir."

"That's 'light' for complexion. Occupation?"

Mr. Nance cleared his throat real quiet. "Rancher."

"The crime of which you were convicted, Mr. Nance?"

"Unlawful cohabitation."

"One of those Mormon cohabs, is that right, Mr. Nance? How many wives you got, sir?"

Mr. Nance didn't say nothing.

"Looks like you know how to keep your mouth shut," said Mr. Norton. "I expect you'll conduct yourself well here, Mr. Nance, seeing as you're not a violent criminal."

"I will," said Mr. Nance.

A guard pulled him by the arm past me. The two of them turned the corner and was gone. A couple more guards come in and pushed by.

Next was the Chinaman, who was standing right in front of me. He just stayed right where he was.

"Prisoner number 87. Name?" said Mr. Norton. He didn't get no answer. He shouted, "Name?"

The man's answer sounded like "Shin Han."

"Yes, well," said Mr. Norton. "So you've learned some English. Isn't that an amazing feat." He grunted again. "Age?"

"Twent-four."

"Height? I'll say five foot six."

I leaned just a little bit around Mr. Han and looked with 'bout one eyeball, and I could sorta see Mr. Norton by that time. He was a mountain of a man, and he was setting behind a desk and writing in a big old book.

"Complexion is olive," said Mr. Norton out loud to hisself while scribbling in his record book. "And no occupation."

But Shin Han said, "Merchant and muse."

Mr. Norton snapped, "'Merchant' I get. What's 'muse'?"

Even with his hands chained up together, and me still looking at his back, I could tell Shin Han was showing he could play a instrument with strings.

"Musician," said Mr. Norton. "Not 'muse.' Musician."

"Yes," said Shin Han. "Musician."

"Well," said Mr. Norton. "We'll expect you to entertain us, Mr. Han. You just better be telling the truth."

Shin Han nodded. "Yes. I tell truth. I play musician."

Grunt. "You were convicted of assault, Mr. Han. You step out of line and you'll end up in the Hole. Do you understand?"

"Yes, sir."

A guard turned him around and pushed him by me just when Mr. Norton said, "Next!"

Being the only one left, I kinda lurched forward into the room. Even though Mr. Norton was setting, he still had to look down at me. "You're Mr. Jake Oliver Evans."

How did he know? I said, "Yes, sir."

He was writing in his big book. "You are now officially prisoner 88 of the Idaho Territorial Penitentiary."

Was I a number now instead of a name? I opened my mouth to ask him, but Mr. Norton, with arms like logs, leaned forward. "Says you're in here for manslaughter. Is that so."

"Yes, sir. Well, that's what they said. . . ."

"I thought this was a mistake," said Mr. Norton, "sending us a kid out here." He picked through some papers and then held one up. "You got five years?"

I lifted my hands with them cuffs on, trying to scratch at my head. I told him, "Ain't no mistake, mister. It's me."

He kinda squinched up his eyes like he didn't much like me. "Height?"

A guard, the one with the orange hair, measured me, using a tall piece of wood. "Four foot six," he said.

Mr. Norton wrote it down. A fly buzzed across the room, and he swatted at it. Then he crossed his arms and looked me clean in the face. "Well, now, where are we supposed to put you?"

"In one of them cells," I said. "Ain't that right?"

"You got a quick mouth, don't you, son?"

I looked at the floor. Pa used to say that, and then he'd knock me good.

Mr. Norton shook his head. "Well, looks like you've got it all figured out, Mr. Jake Oliver Evans."

I told him, "I reckon."

Mr. Norton snorted. "You better hope so." He turned to the orange-haired guard. "For now he's got a fancy room all to himself. On the top, Henry. First cell."

Henry nodded, a bunch of that orange hair flopping around.

I was gonna be on the highest-up place in the building. That was great. I liked looking out and down on things, like when I climbed a barn where Pa and me was supposed to be tending pigs. I fell off the roof and broke this left arm. That's why it don't hang straight. But I seen a long way off from that roof.

Mr. Norton kept on talking. "This place was built for one inmate in a cell. But we have too much lawlessness since the gold rush. We've got twice the bad men we're supposed to have. So you just feel real lucky that you have a cell all to yourself."

"Yes, sir."

"But don't count on that lasting."

"No, sir."

Henry led me by my crooked arm around the corner to a heavy door. He unlocked it and then locked it back up behind us. His ring of keys clinked and my handcuffs clunked when we crossed the dirt yard. It was baked hard as rock from the sun. We walked up three stone steps to a all-white stone building. Then Henry unlocked the door to the cell block and walked me into my new home.

TWO

I smelled some stinky places in my life, like that old pig farm where I fell off the barn roof. But my first whiff of that cell-block like 'bout choked the life outta me. I couldn't see one thing at first, coming in outta the bright sunshine to the black dark. After a couple seconds, though, I could see enough. It weren't much to look at.

A whole big wall of nothing set on one side. Across from it, three rows of cells, one on top of the other. There was thirteen cells in each row. Supposed to hold thirteen and thirteen and thirteen men. That's a whole bunch already, but there was 'bout two times that bunch of stinky bodies in there.

It was hot inside, and it weren't even dead summer yet. But it weren't dry like outside. It felt like a cave, sweaty and sticky, like where me and Pa lived for some days way back when I was little and we didn't have no place else.

There was two cleaning-up cells with tubs and water to wash. But there was a honey bucket cell, too. Nothing you can do to stop that smell when a building's all closed up tight.

The men, they was all wound up, seeing as we was a bunch of new inmates. They was yelling and scraping metal things against the bars and whistling. But when Henry and me walked across toward the steps, all that noise flew away. I felt everybody looking at me. And then one guy yelled, "Look, it's a midget." A couple of 'em laughed, and the noise started right up again.

Henry led me up two sets of steps to my cell on the top. But damn, there was no window looking out. There weren't enough light to hardly see nothing. Alls I coulda looked at anyways was that wall looking right back at me. Couldn't even see much through them flat bars cause they was so tight together. I could barely fit my finger through a hole. A couple windows at the ends of the building let in some sun but showed off a whole lotta nothing else.

"Jake, you're gonna hear the dinner whistle blow soon," said Henry. "Two o'clock every day. No matter where you are, you'll be brought back to your cell to eat."

My stomach let out a roar, and both me and Henry laughed.

"They feed us every day?" I couldn't hardly believe that.

"Every day."

Henry took off my cuffs. My wrists was kinda scraped up,

so I rubbed 'em and licked at the dried-up blood while I watched Henry walk away after locking me in. Before I barely had a chance to take a look around, the dinner whistle blew. The block got quiet. And not a minute later, the block door opened. I could sorta see a lady and a couple of men carrying in metal trays just heaped up with food. They started at the bottom floor, and I knew they was sliding them trays right through slits in the cell doors, just like the one in mine.

I was drooling on myself and 'bout to die when finally the lady come up the steps with a tray. She stood there and stared at me, holding that tray so close I 'bout stuck my tongue through one of them tiny holes. She said, "So you're the young man everybody's talking about."

"Is that my food?"

She smiled and said, "Well, Jake, yes it is. Looks like you could use it."

She slipped the metal tray through the slit in the door, and I stood holding it with both of my hands. I thought for sure I was dreaming. Hunks of beef, little round potatoes, green and white and red beans, cabbage, and two slices of good bread. I set down on the floor and shoved handfuls of food into my mouth, not even bothering with the spoon. I gulped half a tin cup of strong, hot coffee, burped real big, and then used the second piece of bread and scraped up every last scrap on my plate.

"When's the last time you had a nice big meal like that, Jake?" The lady had stood there watching the whole thing.

I licked the metal tray, burped one more time, and wiped my mouth on my sleeve. Then I told her the truth. "I ain't never ate like that before. No, ma'am. Never seen that much food all together under my nose at one time."

She shook her head and then took my tray down the stairs. She come back up the steps a few minutes later and walked by, and I was hoping maybe she forgot she already give me a tray and I'd get another one. No luck.

I reckon all that food kinda knocked me out anyways. I woke up and I was all twisted up in a scratchy old blanket on the bottom metal bunk. I stood up and stretched my arms out and near 'bout touched the two walls in my cell.

A voice I heard before come around the corner at me from the cell next door. "Jake?"

"Yes, sir," I said.

"It's Joshua Nance, Jake. If you'd like to talk, I'll be right here."

I knew that man. "You's the old beard man I come in with."

"That's right, Jake."

I stepped close to the bars. "Why you in here, Mr. Nance? 'Cause you got more than one wife?"

Mr. Nance made a sound like he was losing air. "Something like that."

I couldn't make sense of it. Pa didn't even have one wife since Ma died 'fore I was big enough to remember. So maybe having more than one was good just in case. "But you didn't hurt no one, did you, Mr. Nance?"

"No, Jake. I would never hurt anyone."

"Well, I did. They say I shot somebody, though I don't know that's what I really wanted to do. It just happened." Then I shut up. I didn't feel like talking 'bout it no more with Mr. Nance. I just felt like, I don't know, doing nothing. And that's 'bout what I did 'cept for using the honey bucket cell when Henry come by. Guess I got used to the stink pretty quick 'cause it didn't much bother me no more. Henry asked did I want to wash up. Now that was punishment. "Heck, no," I told him, and went back to my cell and slept right on through 'til daylight.

THREE

Next morning I could hardly believe what I was hearing. It was time to eat again. Walking on down the steps in a line, we men headed through a doorway to the eating room. Some of the men was wearing cuffs, like that Mr. Meecham. But still, I was thinking that in two days I got more food than I ever got in my whole life. Maybe I was in heaven instead of jail.

Breakfast weren't no big meal like supper. We got a bowl of mashed-up stuff—coulda been wheat or barley or tree leaves swimming around in some sorta ooze. I didn't never figure it out exactly. And it was just barely enough to stop starvation for the men who was headed out to do work. But that weren't the worst thing. The worst thing was all us men had to sit together at tables and eat, and we was not allowed to talk. Not one word.

Red Face the guard—turned out his name was Miles—him and his no-talking self fit right in.

I was setting in my spot, shoveling the slop into my mouth. *Nudge.* The man setting next to me jabbed me in the side with his elbow. I just kept on slurping. *Nudge.* There it come again. I give him a look. His eyes was popped out and wide like somebody who seen the devil. He was grinning, and he started giggling, real low and crazy-like.

I'd heard tell 'bout the rule. Oh, I'd heard it good. No talking means no talking. But sometimes a man gets to ya and ya gotta let him have it. My mouth didn't pay no attention to the rules. I looked right at that crazy man and asked, "What are you lookin' at?"

That made him grin even more. And then he quick reached out and grabbed at my throat.

I broke free and jumped up, knocking over my bowl. "You son of a—" But then he had his two hands coming at my neck. I kneed him in the chest. He yelped and doubled on over.

The men was all cheering us on.

"You gawddam loon!" I'd heard Pa use them words, and they seemed like good ones right then. Me and the guy was on the floor, and I believe I was getting the best of him.

And then he spit in my face.

I punched at him, but Miles had me up in the air, my arms behind my back. Henry and another guard had the spitting loon by his arms. And outside the cellblock we all went.

Miles and me, with my arms squeezed into the crook of

one fat elbow, headed for the Warden's Building. The other three went out through the gate. Toward the Hole.

I tried to yank free. "You's hurtin' my arms!"

Miles said nothing and just kept pulling me along.

"Let go!" But he wouldn't let go, and I couldn't get loose.

And then we was in the Warden's Building, and there was the Mountain, setting at that desk, looking down at me again.

"Jake. You haven't even been here one entire day." Mr. Norton set back with his tree-trunk arms crossed over his chest.

Miles let go of me.

I told the Mountain, "He grabbed me." That come out sounding baby-like. "I mean he tried to strangle me."

Still didn't get a rise outta him.

"That man's crazy," I said. "His eyes was gonna pop right outta his head. How come I had to set next to him?"

The Mountain just set there.

I wasn't done. I crossed my own arms. "I coulda took him."

The Mountain picked something out of a back tooth with a twig. Then he opened a big old book on his desk.

"I hope you enjoyed your breakfast, Jake." His face didn't change. He said, "Bread and water, Miles. Three days."

Miles nodded.

"Bread and water?" I couldn't believe it. "That's all that crazy man's gonna get? I thought he was headin' for the Hole."

Mr. Norton smiled and give a jerk of his head like *Get him outta here*. Miles grabbed at my crooked arm, and we was headed on out.

Then I got it. It was me getting just bread and water for three days. Damn.

FOUR

Locked back up in my cell, I walked one end to the other to the other to the other. Couldn't hardly stretch out my legs. All that walking, I got to thinking how Mr. Nance said I could talk to him if need be.

I leaned against the bars. "Mr. Nance? You there?"

I didn't get no answer from him. Instead, a squeaky voice down aways yelled, "He's haulin' wood today, ya little sissy."

That burned me. I'da liked to put that old squeaky-voiced man in my own prison. A secret prison. I imagined him smaller than me and with a head of nothing but mouth.

You ain't even gettin' bread, you old Mouth. You just stay on in there and rot.

And then I felt a whole lot better.

* * *

Every day after dinner, we men was supposed to have ninety minutes out in the yard, rain or shine, that's what they said.

Well, the next day, for the first time in 'bout a year, it rained so hard like to float the penitentiary clean away. Had to wait it out. Finally the rain stopped and the sun come out and so did we.

Mr. Nance, his beard all shaved off, stood close by me. And that Chinaman, Shin Han, he weren't far off neither. Men was talking and moving around in the mud, and somebody pulled out a mouth organ. He was a tall, skinny guy, way skinnier than even me. Heard him called Slim. He played a tune I'd heard before, kinda light and happy.

I started out walking around the inside of that high wall, dragging my fingers along the stone and then the wood section, going nowhere in particular but forward. 'Fore I knew it, there was a guy walking along behind me. We was just walking in a great big square, the ground drying out in the sun. Then I seen a beetle bug swimming in a puddle ahead and I reached down to look closer and the guy run right into me.

"Damn kid." He kinda kicked at me while I was hunched on over. "What're you doin' in here anyway?"

I stood up, and the guy punched me with his fist, right in my gut.

There weren't no air left in me, and my throat closed up tight. I flapped my arms like I was trying to fly, but really I was just trying to breathe.

Then Henry was there, had the guy's arms pinned behind him and was hauling him across the yard.

Mr. Nance was looking on, but I was sucking at the air and couldn't get enough to talk to nobody.

I got a bunch of looks from the other men who was talking then, but they wasn't talking 'bout me. They was talking 'bout what was gonna happen to the guy that punched me.

"Gonna lose five good days," I heard.

"Ain't enough for solitary."

"Wanna bet? See what Norton says."

Finally, I got a whole big breath. Stars was flying around in front of my eyes.

"Walk it off," said Mr. Nance.

Shin Han nodded at me and started out. I walked along with him.

I tried my voice. It sounded kinda rough, but it was still there. "You hurt somebody, Mr. Han? That why you in here?" I rubbed at my punched belly.

Shin Han didn't answer right away. But then he said, "Protect my store."

"Was someone robbing you?"

"Yes. Drunk man, mean man."

"A Chinaman?"

He nodded.

"Is he in here?"

Shin Han shook his head. "I hit back. He take away quick. Step in front of horse."

"The horse run him down?"

21

He nodded again, and we kept on walking.

"I tell secret, Jake," said Shin Han.

I said, "Don't know I'm good at keeping secrets, but I'll try."

"In China, Shin is last name. No Han."

I got it. "So you's Mr. Shin, not Mr. Han. Is that right?"

He nodded and smiled and we walked two more times around inside that whole big fence, and then it was time to go back in. We all dragged our damp selves across the yard, and I was ready to head on up to my cell and take me a nap. But then there come the Mountain, heading straight for me.

"Jake," said Mr. Norton. "Warden Johnson would like to see you in his office."

The warden. Damn.

"Yes, sir," I said. But I'm thinking if they take away my bread and water, I might as well just curl up in the corner and die.

FIVE

Henry was standing right there beside the Mountain. He didn't cuff me or nothing. Then we three men just hiked on over to see the warden. We was through the door and walking loud together down the wood hallway, like marching, on into the Mountain's office, past his desk, and right on up to the warden's door.

The Mountain knocked. I heard a quiet voice from inside, not a loud hollering voice like I expected. But my heart was jumping around in my chest anyways. The Mountain cleared his giant throat, opened the door, and let me and Henry walk past him and right on in.

An old man was setting at the warden's desk. His long white beard and mustache was so bushy they looked like snow animals.

"Jake," said White Beard, "I'm Warden Johnson."

I asked, "Are you sure?"

He laughed, and I could see that Henry was kinda smiling, too. The Mountain just stood there.

"Yes, Jake, I'm certain that I am Warden Johnson."

"I just thought maybe you'd be bigger."

He nodded toward the Mountain. "You mean bigger than Mr. Norton?"

I didn't really know what I meant. My face sorta stung.

"There aren't many men who are bigger than Mr. Norton, Jake. Around here, that's a good thing, don't you think?"

I decided I would agree with everything he said. I nodded my head a good long time.

"You're not in trouble this time, Jake. I assume that's what you were thinking on your walk over here."

I was nodding the truth then.

"The man who punched you will serve time in solitary. Five days. And he will not be allowed in the yard with the other inmates for a while."

"Why'd he do that?" I asked. "Why'd he punch me? Alls I was doing was looking at a bug."

"I don't know why men do a lot of the things they do. It's easy for a grown man, a coward like him, to pick on someone like you. And that's what we were afraid might happen."

Afraid?

White Beard kept talking. "When we got your court papers, we thought your age was written down wrong. We really aren't set up here to house someone like you."

"But I got my own place now. And food. . . ."

"Two more days, Jake, and you'll get that dinner tray back."

I couldn't help myself. "That breakfast man, he deserved that, Warden."

"Rules are rules, Jake. And punishment is punishment." He tugged at his beard. "Two days will go by quickly."

I kept my mouth shut and nodded again.

"Don't worry about food," he said. "The governor will see to it that you will always have your meals."

Then I was real confused. "But I don't know the governor."

"No, Jake. But he has set up a fund—money to pay the expenses for young offenders who have no other support."

No other support. "I guess Pa don't have nothing to give."

"It doesn't matter, Jake," said White Beard. "You will eat."

And then I didn't know if I should ask, but I did anyways. "Is Pa coming around here? To see me?"

Warden Johnson smoothed the whiskers around his mouth. "You're a pretty tough kid, Jake. I think it's only fair to tell you that it's unlikely."

"So," I said, "he won't be waiting around for me when I get out."

A big old silence filled up the room. Then I remembered. "Hey, I got five years in here. I'll be growed up by then."

"Yes, well," said the warden. "I'm not sure you'll be in here for the full five years."

They was gonna throw me out on my own. Figured.

"We don't know how long you'll be here, Jake, but I will keep you informed." He cleared his throat sorta lady-like. "Jake, have you had any schooling?"

"Me? No, sir. Don't know as I ever seen a school."

"There's an inmate here who has volunteered to teach you."

"Teach me what?"

This time he smoothed his whole beard. "Teach you to read."

I let out a snort. "I'm too dumb to read." That's what Pa always said.

"That might not be true, Jake. So you will work with Brother Nance each afternoon."

"Does Brother Nance know Mr. Nance?"

White Beard smiled. "They're the same man, Jake. Some of us call him Brother Nance, out of respect."

"But wait, if y'all respect him, how come he's in here?"

"Laws," he said. "Laws are laws."

"So. . . ." I was trying to make sense outta all that. "He broke a law, but he didn't really hurt no one, and he's a good man."

"That's about right. And he's willing to work with you, to teach you to read."

It weren't like I had a load of other stuff to do around there. "Okay. What am I gonna read?"

"I assume you'll start with the Bible. But we will be acquiring a few more books and starting a library here one of these days. Idle hands and minds lead to trouble, Jake."

"Like that trouble this afternoon," I said.

White Beard was looking off somewheres past me. "That's right. It's tough keeping them all busy right now, even with the stone work."

I had to know. "What stone work?"

"On top of the hill, Jake, just below Table Rock. They're cutting the sandstone to finish the fence, to replace the wood."

They was working up high on them hills.

"I can cut up stone," I said.

White Beard shook his head. "It's too dangerous, Jake. They use dynamite."

Dynamite? "Who uses dynamite?"

White Beard stared off again. "The inmates assigned to the quarry use the dynamite, Jake. We can't afford to pay outsiders. It's not an ideal situation, but you've seen the wall. It's coming along." He nodded. "But the men are going to have more work once the orchard is planted and the crops are put in. Right now all we've got to tend to is hogs and—"

"I worked with hogs a while back."

The Mountain stepped in front of me and looked down hard. "Don't interrupt the warden."

I stared at my old boots.

Warden Johnson said, "You worked with hogs? Is that right? Well then, you'll give Mr. Criswell a hand."

Me and my big mouth.

SIX

Next morning Henry come up early to my cell. He handed me two thick slices of bread with lard. I tore into them.

"I'm to walk you over to the hogs now," he said.

I didn't mind one bit walking right past that eating room, even if the other men was already gone.

Me and Henry started out. The air felt nice and cool 'cause it was early. But it was gonna be hot, I could tell. We hiked 'bout a mile or so, up a rise and down a rise and around past some scraggly old trees, 'til we got to the hogs. Wasn't no wind blowing, so I didn't know I was there 'til I was there.

It didn't smell nothing like that other hog farm me and Pa worked. It weren't bad at all.

We stood at the fence that surrounded the pen. A sea of mostly black hogs moved around inside, grunting and snuffling. One of them headed on over to me, sticking its snout through the fence, giving me a sniff. Then it went for my boot lace. I hopped up to the middle slat of the fence and stepped sideways along the rail, but that hog kept right on after my lace.

"You break it, you fix it."

I jumped on down and stepped away from the fence. And there come the man who said those words. He was shuffling alongside the fence, all slumped over at the shoulders, like he was looking permanent at the ground. He stopped right in front of me and Henry.

Henry said to the top of the man's head, "This here's Jake, Mr. Criswell."

Mr. Criswell bent his whole body back to look me up and down. His right young-looking face didn't match with his bent-over self. His eyes was the same blue as the sky.

"You break that fence rail, you fix it. Don't make work, Jake," said Mr. Criswell.

"Yes, sir."

We three men just stood looking for a minute—Henry and me at the hogs, Mr. Criswell at a spot between his feet.

He said, "Just looks like a whole bunch of pigs, doesn't it, Jake?"

"Yes, sir," I said, 'cause it *was* just a whole bunch of pigs.

He said, "That's a lot of cooking fat and pork meat." He pointed over the fence past the heap of pig bodies. "That fella there is our boar."

I couldn't miss him. He was covered in bristly hair, mostly black with some white patches. He stood in a small pen all to hisself, and he was bigger than the bathtub in the washing cell.

Mr. Criswell said, "There's six sows and forty-five good-sized pigs."

I didn't know what to say 'bout that. I couldn't count up that high, so I hoped that weren't what he was getting at.

Mr. Criswell was chewing on a piece of straw. "I was told you know your way around a hog, Jake."

Why did I have to go and say that? "Well, me and Pa worked a couple days on a hog farm. Pa did some shoveling and cleaning up. But mostly I . . ."

I coulda maybe made something up, but I figured Mr. Criswell could tell I didn't know nothing 'bout hogs.

"I mostly played with a big old cat that hung around. And I fell off the roof of the barn."

Mr. Criswell seemed like he was nodding in agreement, or maybe his head just sorta bounced up and down a little bit all by itself when he laughed.

"An expert," he said.

I was thinking, *Shut your smart mouth*, but my gut knew he was right.

"Get yourself a shovel there." He pointed off a ways.

Henry said, "Looks like you're set, Jake." And then right after he took off, I seen a scrawny old yellow gold cat chasing after him. I looked away from that cat so fast I 'bout snapped my own neck. No more cats and no more roofs.

I found myself a shovel and a wheelbarrow that looked and smelled like it rode a lot of manure around in it. Mr. Criswell opened the gate and walked on into that sea of pigs. They rubbed up against his legs and gave off little snorting noises. In the middle of the big pen, a short stone wall run through, cutting the pen in two. A small wood slat gate led to the other side.

"We gotta move 'em through the gate to the other side to clean up. Get on in here and give me a hand."

I set down the shovel and went on in. My first step inside and I looked down at my boot in a pile of pig shit. I was gonna be wearing that smell on my boots forever. "Damn."

"Watch your mouth," said Mr. Criswell. "Hogs are smart. They pretty much know where to do their business. But sometimes they make a mistake. And there's no way to work around hogs without getting some of that mistake on you."

The pigs swarmed around me, snuffling and poking at me. "How do we get these here pigs moving?" I asked.

"Well, most of them are interested in people, Jake, so they'll just follow us."

I worked my way through the crowd toward Mr. Criswell, and sure enough, the pigs was following. And then the one that had went after my laces, he was at it again. He was black with a white spot shaped like a egg on his back, and if I hadn't started moving so fast, Egg the hog woulda ate that lace right outta my boot. I tripped my way into the other side of the pen.

Mr. Criswell shuffled in behind me and then so did Egg and all the other hogs. 'Cept one. That one just stood there facing the other way, waving its tail at me, showing me its rump.

"That one's stubborn," said Mr. Criswell, shutting us and all the rest of the pigs in the clean side. "You go on over there and bring her in."

I stood still, hoping maybe Mr. Criswell might change his mind, but then Egg started in on my laces again. So I quick stepped through the gate, closing it behind me.

That stubborn pig had wandered on to the far end of the pen near the wallow. I didn't want to go there, so I lifted my foot and made them laces flap. Thought maybe she'd go for 'em just like Egg.

Nothing.

So I stepped on over and flapped them laces right in front of Miss Rump's big old stubborn pig face.

Nothing again.

"Come on, piggy," I said. I whistled and clapped my hands and started running back toward the other pigs. Still nothing. So I got behind that pig and give her a shove. She backed into me, and down I went. The wet soaked in through the seat of my pants.

I was mad. "You dang old pig. Get moving." I pinched her with all my strength, right on that muddy rump. She sprung ahead, running around in circles, and I was running around after her 'til finally she was headed straight for the gate. Mr.

Criswell just stood there, and I thought for sure there would be a collision. But at the last second, he opened the gate and that mean old sow strolled right on in.

I give Rump my best evil eye, but she was already trotting to a nice clean patch of hay.

Seat of my pants dried kinda stiff while we mucked out the used side. I never done so much shoveling in my whole life. Manure's heavy. And my crooked arm had some trouble holding that shovel and then got to shaking the more I worked. We cleaned up that side. Well, it weren't what you'd call clean really. It was just sorta plain dirt at that point.

Another wheelbarrow was for hauling straw and hay and dried-up grasses. I filled that thing I don't know how many times, and we tossed that dried stuff all around so's that side would be ready tomorrow.

"Time to eat," said Mr. Criswell. Even with all that smell and dirt around me, my mouth started watering.

I said, "I didn't know that was part of this here job."

His head bobbed. "I didn't mean it's time for us to eat. It's time for the hogs."

But I was hungry. Two more days I was going without real food. I blurted out, "I'm on bread and water for three days."

Mr. Criswell bent back and looked at me. "What did you do?"

I weren't gonna sound like a baby this time. "I punched a guy at the breakfast table. A big guy. He'd grabbed me round my neck."

"What happened to him?"

"He's in the Hole for five days."

"You planning on punching anybody else any time soon?"

I never planned to punch nobody. "No, sir," I said. And then he shared some beef jerky he had in his pocket.

After that, I just done whatever he said, no questions at all. We mixed up grains and what looked like dried-up bits of maybe some sorta cooked-up animal parts with some water from a rain barrel, and we slopped them hogs.

'Fore I knew it, Henry was back at the fence. "Where's Mr. Criswell?"

Seemed like he done snuck off when I was feeding them pigs. But then we seen him doing his shuffling from the shed with a bundle of something in his hands.

"Afternoon, Henry," he said.

"Afternoon, Mr. Criswell. Everything okay?"

"Looks like it," he said. "Jake, you change on into these clothes." He handed me britches and a shirt. "These here boots are gonna be big on you."

I took them clothes and went to the shed to change. The boots were my foot and another set of toes longer, but they was nicer made than any I'd ever had.

Mr. Criswell hollered, "Hang those dirty ones on that peg. You wear them when you're working."

I come on out. Henry kinda smiled when he seen my too-big clothes and especially the boots.

Mr. Criswell said, "Don't go getting into any fights with the other men over those clothes."

I nodded. For a while there I had almost forgot where I lived.

SEVEN

Henry and me started walking back in the sun. We wasn't saying nothing 'cause that hot day I knew was coming had wrapped itself around us. My new clothes was heavier than the old ones, and the boots tried to jump off. And I ain't never worked that much, so I was sweating like I was gonna melt.

I thought 'bout them pigs. Some of them was okay, kinda friendly, like a pet. I was thinking how it'd be nice to have one of them for my own. But I seen how big they get. Couldn't hardly fit me and one of them full-growed hogs in my cell together.

Henry snapped me out of my daydreaming. He said, "You're gonna work with Brother Nance starting this afternoon, Jake."

I had nothing to say to that. I'd rather muck out pigpens all day long than learn reading.

We was in sight of the round-top wood gate when the dinner whistle blew. I tried running, but them boots made me wobbly.

"Hold up, Jake," yelled Henry. "They won't forget to feed you."

And he was right. Got my meal right on time. Three pieces of bread instead of two. The food lady—her name was Mrs. Ayres—she musta made a mistake. I sucked the last bits of bread outta my teeth, setting on my bunk, leaning back against the stone wall. Then I changed into my only other set of clothes. They was full of holes, but they mostly fit. I set back down and thought I'd finally take a real long look around my space.

Bricks on the floor, three stone walls, and that too-tight-wove metal door. A cage. I stood up and walked the length of my cage. Six not-angry steps long and then 'bout four wide.

So far I'd only slept on the low bunk, so I hoisted myself on up to the high one. Room enough to set up all right, but I guess I'd knowed that ceiling was gonna make it a too-small place for me to think. I quick hopped down and stretched out on my sleeping bunk. And then I figured out what I'd do with that high-up piece. I'd put my secret prison up there, put that squeaky-voice man in it. *You get on up there, you Mouth. And you ain't getting no food at all.* Glad I finally had a place to put him.

Then I thought maybe I'd put something nice up there, too, in its own separate place. A nice-looking piggy, not too big. Named her Emma. She wouldn't get no bigger and she wouldn't stink up the place and she didn't need to eat. She'd just hang around sleeping all day, waiting for me to close my eyes and drift on up and say howdy.

'Fore I knew it, Henry unlocked my cage and we headed next door.

"Hello, Jake," said Mr. Nance.

The other man in the cell set on his up-high bunk, legs hanging down off the side, and kept on reading silent to hisself.

A book and a piece of slate and chalk set next to Mr. Nance on his bunk. "Time for your first reading lesson, son."

Henry give me a look when he locked the door. It was a shrug and a eyebrow raise that said something like *Maybe it won't be as tough as you think.*

Yeah, what did he know.

I set down next to Mr. Nance, and I could see some writing on that slate already.

Mr. Nance seen me looking. "Do you know what letter that is, Jake?"

I don't know how I knew it, but I did. "That's a *A*, Mr. Nance."

He looked kinda shocked. "Well, I was prepared to start right from the beginning, Jake, but it looks like you already have a start on your letters."

"Yeah, well, don't get too happy 'cause I think that's 'bout it." And I was right. I still don't know how I figured out that letter *A*.

We worked on letters *B* and *C* and started on *D*, but I was withering after all that hog business.

"Come on, Jake. Work on the letter *D*, and then I can show you a word that you can read."

So I kept at that chalk. *A, B, C, D*. A few more times. My letters looked shaky and uneven-like, but I got 'em down.

"Now what's that word you say I can read, Mr. Nance?"

He took the chalk and wrote B-A-D. "Your first word, Jake. Do you know what it says?"

"No, sir."

"Say the sounds."

"Buh, ay, duh."

"Now put them together." He give me a second to think, but nothing hit me. So he told me, "That word is 'bad.'"

"Bad," I said. My first whole word was 'bad.' Now in a place like that, didn't that just make sense.

Mr. Nance knew what I was thinking. "I didn't start with that word on purpose, Jake. It just happens to be a word that I can make out of the letters you learned."

"Sure, Mr. Nance, I see."

He had me write that word a few times, 'til I 'bout passed out.

"It'll get better, Jake."

Mr. Nance went on then and read a passage from his Book of Mormon to me, but it went flowing right on through my head.

Next thing I knew, I woke up in the total dark in my own cell. I heard snoring all down through the block, so I went right on back to sleep.

EIGHT

My second day to work the hogs, Henry come to get me since I still weren't eating the morning meal with the others. But I couldn't move. Every muscle in every place on me said, *No sir, we ain't moving*. Blisters on my hands had opened, and the ooze had crusted up.

"I ain't going," I said.

Henry didn't budge.

I turned over on my bunk and pretended like I was still sleeping. I could feel him standing there. I still don't remember getting dressed, but I ended up shoveling again that day, hoping all them hogs would fall down dead and I could go on back and sleep.

I got my food tray again after my three days. I think I musta growed two inches right after that, so them bigger clothes started fitting.

Every morning from then on, Henry walked me on over to the hogs. Either I was getting stronger or there weren't so much manure to shovel up.

I believed it was just me and Mr. Criswell working them hogs. But one day, after a couple of weeks, I found out I was wrong 'bout that.

"You stole my boots."

A boy 'bout a head taller than me, with black hair flying out in all directions, stood right in front of me while I scooped a big shovel full of hog mess. I never seen where he come from.

"You stole my job, too. This here was my job."

I blinked hard. Maybe the sun was playing tricks.

"Ma said a man from the pen was working the hogs. You ain't no man."

My lips was sealed up real tight so's I wouldn't go and say something wrong.

He kept on. "What you in for? Somebody look at you and laugh himself to death?"

I dropped my shovel. Just when my mouth was deciding what to say, Mr. Criswell come from the shed.

"Jake, this is Charles. My son. He used to do your job. But you're here now, and after the summer, he'll be going to school."

I 'bout saw smoke coming from Charles's ears.

"He'll still help out from time to time, when he's not needed for other chores or when he's off from school. Isn't that right, Charles?"

Charles spit. "He isn't a man."

"And because you're twelve, you think you are?" asked Mr. Criswell. Charles turned and walked off.

At least I knew where my clothes and boots come from.

"He said I stole his boots. Is that true?"

"You didn't steal anything, Jake. I gave those to you, and Charles knew that."

I seen Charles again later, lurking around giving me that same evil eye I give Rump. But I weren't giving him his job back. It was my job now. I was 'specially sure 'bout that the next day, 'cause I had to miss.

I was eating my breakfast slop at the table, setting as far from every man as possible, like I always did. The stone-quarry men started off. Some of the others who cleaned the kitchen or chopped firewood or done laundry, they set off, too. But Henry weren't there like usual to walk me to Mr. Criswell's.

I asked Miles, "Is Henry late?"

He shook his head. "Sick" is all he said.

"Well, who's gonna take me to the hogs?" I asked.

The Mustache, whose real name was Len, said, "Not today. We don't got no guard to walk with ya."

"But who's gonna do my work?" And then I knew who would do my work. I jumped up. "I gotta go. That's my job!"

Len said, "You want to get writ up in the punishment record book for back talkin'?"

"What? I just want to get to my job."

"One more word." And then I knew there weren't nothing I could do. I was gonna set locked up in my cell all day 'til dinner, and Charles was gonna take away my job.

Back in my cage, I set on my bunk, thinking 'bout not thinking. I decided I'd close my eyes and fly on up to the upper bunk and visit Emma. Before I done that, I put Charles in with the Mouth, and they was having some sorta altercation. I made sure to lock up that part of my secret room.

So me and Emma was just floating on some clouds, chewing on straw, when I near 'bout jumped outta my skin.

BOOM!! The whole block shook. And then the men who was left in their cells set up a holler. "Yippee!"

Was they cheering for the world to end? Mr. Nance and his cell mate wasn't next door to ask. So I kept my hands over my ears and I curled up tight. I laid like that 'til all my muscles ached.

Finally I set up. The building hadn't fallen on my head, but maybe it still would. I had to think, so I got up and started pacing. Back and forth for a real long time. Then I tried to climb up the metal door. Don't know where I thought I was going, just trying to move to someplace different. But my feet slipped on that metal. I went down hard on my backside and then went on back to pacing with a sorta limp.

No more explosions, so I tried to think 'bout Emma again, but that was wrecked.

I laid down on the cool floor.

I stood upside down on my hands.

I picked at a scab on my elbow 'til it bled.

And then I cried. Not like anybody coulda heard, but the water just come pouring out, running down under my chin and dripping on the floor. And then I didn't have nothing else I could do but close up my head and sleep.

The dinner whistle woke me up. Mrs. Ayres brung my tray.

"Ms. Ayres, what was that—I mean I heard . . ."

"That boomin' noise, Jake?"

I really did hear it.

She explained the whole thing, and I laughed like I'd knowed it all along.

"Nobody's really in charge when the men and guards go up to the stone quarry," she said. "They're supposed to blast the rock just enough to loosen it up. They load the big pieces on the wagon and roll them down here and cut the stones clean to finish building the outside wall."

Then Mrs. Ayres moved as close to my ear as she could on the other side of the door. She whispered, "Sometimes the men get in their minds to use all of the dynamite at one time. I've heard tell they dig a bunch of holes and stuff it all in. Then they light the fuse and run like the dickens." Her fingers opened wide beside her face. "Boom," she said, kinda quiet.

So that's what I heard. The rock getting blasted into tiny little bits, not any of 'em good for wall building. The men got yelled at, but they'd say the dynamite was bad, and the guards didn't know any better. They'd all come on back down with a empty wagon, and their work was done for that day.

At least the men had got out. But I quit feeling sorry for myself when I found out what happened to Henry. He missed a day 'cause he had a bad tooth. The next day he was back. Looked like he had a cheek full of nuts, like a big old squirrel. And he sounded like his mouth was stuffed full of cloth. "Tha barber din know what he wath doin'. Wook." He pulled his lip to the side, and I seen a swole-up mess. "It boke." And I could see there was still a piece of tooth there where it weren't supposed to be. "So now I got ta go back." He winced.

My mouth started to hurt, too, but weren't nothing I could do to help him. He took me on to my job, holding the side of his face all the way there. Mr. Criswell seen him coming and took him on over to his house to get him some medicine. Smelled like whiskey on his way back past.

My job was still mine, and I was right happy 'bout that. I could see where Charles thought he done cleaned up better'n me. *You wait*, I thought. *I'll show you.*

NINE

'Cause I had to, I kept at that reading stuff. Tough work for me, but I started through the alphabet with a lotta encouraging by Mr. Nance. 'Bout that time, he received in the mail a little book called *The New England Primer*. Found out that my first read word, "bad," was a word with one syllable. Some other words like that was "good" and "job" and "beef" and "cat." And then Mr. Nance wrote a real good word in one syllable: Jake. Practiced that one on my own using my finger and the air.

One day Mr. Nance read a lesson to me. Went like this:

> *Thou shalt not see thy brother's ox or his sheep go*
> *astray, and hide thyself from them; thou shalt in*
> *any case bring them again unto thy brother.*
> *And if thy brother be not nigh unto thee, or thou*
> *know him not, then thou shalt bring it unto thine*
> *own house, and it shall be with thee until thy brother*
> *seek after it, and thou shalt restore it to him again.*

"That's a whole lotta 'thee' and 'thy' and 'thou,'" I said.

Mr. Nance smiled. "What do you think it means, Jake?"

"Well, seems to me like if I had a brother and he had a ox or sheep that wandered on over to my house, I should keep that sheep in my house 'til my brother comes back from nigh. Wherever nigh is."

A great big laugh erupted out of Mr. Nance. Got me to laughing, too. Mr. Nance's cellmate, Mr. Hawkes, jumped down off his bunk and said, "That's enough of that. This boy needs to learn some manners."

Even before that I didn't much like Mr. Hawkes. He didn't never smile, and out in the yard when we all got to talk some, he said Mr. Nance weren't teaching me right 'bout reading. Said I should hear more 'bout religion first, then do the reading part. I was glad he weren't my teacher.

On the Fourth of July, though, we didn't read that day. It was time to celebrate America's birthday.

We was a bunch of men from a whole bunch of different countries. Us born in America felt like just 'cause we was locked up didn't mean we wasn't happy 'bout the whole country's independence. But some of the men was born in places like Scotland or Spain or France or China, and they didn't much care what the celebration was 'bout, as long as there was celebrating.

We was let into the yard for some extra hours that day. We sung songs while one of the men played a fiddle and Slim played his mouth harp. A couple of the men did some dancing. One looked like his pants was on fire. And we all got fresh-baked pies in the late afternoon. Apple and rhubarb with cinnamon.

Some other places had fireworks for their Fourth of July celebration. We didn't need fireworks just one day of the year. We had the stone-quarry men.

Some new men had come in since me. One of them was a Chinaman, Mr. Wu, who took turns playing music with Mr. Shin on a Chinese banjo he brung with him. It was a little round-like instrument with a long skinny neck and three strings. The belly on it was made outta gray snakeskin. Mr. Shin plucked at the strings and started sorta singing. But it weren't like no singing I ever heard. At first I thought that Chinese music sounded like a cat playing that banjo and singing. But then after a while I kinda didn't mind so much. And the banjo was a pretty thing, too, so I put one of them in the good side of my secret room. But without no strings on it.

My days was mostly 'bout the same once I become a old-timer. Tending to the hogs, reading with Mr. Nance, sneaking a pat on the head of that old yellow gold cat when Mr. Criswell weren't around, eating a heaped-up tray of food every darned day, and learning to sleep with all that coughing and snoring and farting going on. I was settled in just fine.

And then that first batch of piggies come along.

TEN

August 13, 1885

I stood shoveling every last bit of pig waste from a spot in the pen. "That sow is acting funny," I told Mr. Criswell. The sow was making noises like I never heard before. Snorting and screeching and almost barking like a dog.

Mr. Criswell's head nodded, so I was being laughed at, or something was funny. He said, "It's time for you to see where piggies come from, Jake."

I had me a idea of where they come from, and I didn't want nothing to do with all that.

"Henry's going to bring you on back here late tonight."

I asked, "Does he know that?"

"He knew it was going to happen eventually. Tonight is the night."

"What are we gonna do in the dark?"

"Well, you know we have lanterns, so we won't be in the total dark."

Maybe I'd drain the oil from the lantern so I wouldn't have to see what he wanted me to see.

"Piggies come in the night or the wee morning hours, Jake," said Mr. Criswell. "This is your job. You be here in case I need help."

Walking home, I thought maybe the sow would finish before I got back that night.

I was wrong.

"Wake up, Jake." Henry held a lantern over my face. Snoring sounds filled the dark. I slipped on my clothes and fumbled into my boots, and we headed out on our midnight walk to the hogs. Before we even got to the pen, I heard that sow making noise. Then she made one sharp pig holler. It echoed off the hills.

I seen Mr. Criswell's lantern in the distance, in the clean side of the pen. In the other side, the rest of the pigs sounded restless—half sleeping, half awake, half stirred up.

"She's about ready, Jake," said Mr. Criswell. "Henry, you come on back tomorrow at the usual time."

"Yes, sir," he said, and him and his lantern headed back. And I realized I weren't going home that whole night.

It got real quiet. The sow weren't making noise no more. She was moving straw, piling it up. She'd go to piss and then come back to push that straw some more. Kept on going and coming back for a long time, 'til I thought there weren't no way she could go one more time. And then she slow went over on her side and laid that wide body down.

"Come on to this end, Jake." Mr. Criswell stood with the lantern at the back end of that sow. So that's where I stood, too. We stood and watched a lot of nothing going on. The sow's thick skin shimmied. She shifted herself a little, then settled back in.

I don't know how long we stood there. Seemed like hours. Wasn't nothing to this having piggies. And then everything started real quick.

Some watery-looking blood shot out at her back end, and then *slip*, out come a little thing, black and wet, with a tiny little tail straight as a stick. That little piggy stayed hooked up to the sow with a string-like piece.

"That's the cord, Jake. They'll all have their own cord."

I asked, "How come its tail don't curl up? All the hogs I seen have curly tails."

"That's the way they come out," said Mr. Criswell. "It'll curl up later."

That little thing moved just slight, like it was waiting patient for the others. We waited, too. Maybe ten or twenty minutes or so, and then *slip*, out come another one, just exact like the first one.

My mouth was so dry, my tongue was gonna crack. Guess my mouth flapped open with that first piggy and stayed flapped. I went and got a dipper of water. Drank down three in a row and then went back to the lantern light.

Them little things took their time. By the time the last one, number seven, come out, I was setting down.

"How come they's just layin' there, Mr. Criswell?"

"They won't start to eat until the afterbirth comes out. Sometimes that takes a while."

He was way right 'bout that. I dozed off some. He kept on poking at me with his boot toes. And then finally here come the nastiest sack of bloody ooze, like some animal without no bones. Mr. Criswell stepped on up and used his knife to cut the cords and tie them up, and then them piggies started squirming. Worked their way right on up to the line of teats across that big sow body and started suckling. They all wanted that first teat. But they moved on back 'til they was all attached, 'cept one. It still wanted that first teat, but that was already taken.

"Why don't that one move on back?"

"Instinct," said Mr. Criswell.

"Or it ain't too smart," I said.

The lantern shadow shifted when Mr. Criswell's head nodded. "They are smart, Jake."

"So that one will figure out there's more to drink from back there," I said.

"More than likely, but you can't tell until a day or two. Now help me with the cleaning up."

I mostly kept my eyes closed when he hauled away that bloodied-up straw and then put down more fresh.

"Gotta keep them real warm in that straw," he said.

It was a nice warm night, so I reckoned we was safe that way. I reached down for one more handful of clean straw, and the next thing I knew, the sun was trying to bake me.

Mr. Criswell was hovering near the sow. I stood up quick.

"I didn't mean to sleep, Mr. Criswell."

He didn't say nothing. I moved closer to the sow and counted the piggies. And then, since my counting weren't too good, I tried it again.

"They's only six piggies."

Mr. Criswell still didn't say nothing. And then, "One got underneath," he said. "I couldn't watch the whole time."

"Underneath?" Oh, lord. Crushed underneath that big sow mama. 'Cause I couldn't stay awake. I grabbed at my head.

Mr. Criswell said, "It's nature, Jake. We got six nice piggies."

All the baby pigs was on the move. They knew right when that milk started to run. But then I saw that the not-smart one was still trying to get to that first teat. "Why ain't he going back to drink?"

"Just the way it is, Jake. Can't change nature."

I didn't care 'bout nature. I was gonna get that piggy to drink from a different teat. That one weren't gonna die on me, too.

I got on my knees and picked that little pig up in my hands. It was powerful strong for such a little runt. I crawled on my knees and set that piggy on a teat back from the others. The runt squirmed its way back to the front. I picked it up again, and again it moved toward the front. The milk time ended, and the sow and piggies slept.

Every time the milk come again, I was right there with that runt. I don't know how long that went on. The sun moved across the sky. I thought maybe I would drop over, but I never did. Slapped my own face to keep on going. One piggy already died 'cause I fell asleep.

I was wearing that runt down. I set it one more time in that back place to drink. That time, it didn't try to jump forward. It set sorta dazed, and I pulled that teat out toward its little pig mouth. A drop of milk leaked out onto its tiny snout. That musta done it. It took a light hold onto its mama, and then it took a strong hold. And it quick sucked up its breakfast and dinner for that whole day.

ELEVEN

The next few days, I watched them piggies grow so fast into hogs, it was almost like after they ate, they puffed up and stayed that much bigger right in front of my face.

A few days after them piggies was born, Charles was at the hogs in the morning. We three just worked quiet, keeping our distance. Me and Charles was raking up every last piece of straw, trying to outdo the other in clean.

Breaking up that quiet, Mr. Criswell said, "Butchering time is coming up, Jake. I'll get some help from a couple of the men." Me and Charles kinda glanced each other's way. We didn't need no other men to help us with nothing. But then, even though that pork meat was just fine, I weren't sure 'bout that butchering stuff. I didn't want to think 'bout that, so my brain changed its direction and my mouth blurted out something that I had been thinking 'bout. "How come you's kinda bent over, Mr. Criswell?"

Charles shot me a look.

"Just an accident, Jake," said Mr. Criswell. "I fell off a horse about three years ago. Broke my back. That's all."

Charles was raking faster.

"Just a pure accident, Jake. Things like that happen."

Then Charles threw down his rake and walked off.

I kept on working, being real exact cleaning out my spot, 'cause then I knew that Charles had something to do with Mr. Criswell's bent back.

I didn't see Charles again 'til I got me a drink. And then there he was at the pump.

"My pa is none of your darn business."

I took another drink of water.

He said, "None of your darn business what happened to make him bent like that."

I stood looking.

And then Charles said, "At least I didn't kill nobody."

In one second we was chest to chest. I blew in his face, "You don't know nothing 'bout what I done."

"You killed a man, I know that." Charles pushed me away.

"What did you do to your pa?" I asked, using my own evil eye. "You shove him off that horse?"

He come at me. I stepped aside real quick and he fell face-down to the ground. He got up and come at me again.

"That's enough," said Mr. Criswell, stepping between us.

Me and Charles stood breathing like horses been running too long.

"You boys keep this up, and neither one of you will ever work the hogs again."

Hung my head. "Sorry, sir." Couldn't hardly believe how much it would hurt not having that job no more. I would not let my mouth take over me in front of Mr. Criswell ever again.

Charles said, "I'm sorry, Pa." And him and me just went on working and wondering.

Just 'bout then, Henry showed up. Him and Mr. Criswell had a few words, and then me and Henry headed on back.

I was kicking up a extra cloud of dust walking along, humming just a bunch of notes.

Henry asked, "You doing okay, Jake?"

"Well, sure," I said. "Mr. Criswell and the hogs are just fine to work with. That dinner whistle is somethin' real special, too. And I ain't got punched in the stomach of late."

Then he asked, "How's that reading coming along?"

I'd like to have told him the truth, that it was just a big old waste of Mr. Nance's time. But that wouldn'ta sounded nice. So I told him, "Reckon I 'bout got my letters down."

As I was saying that, I realized that maybe I *did* have my letters down, and I could even read a word or two more than "bad."

And that's when the old yellow gold cat pounced out from a tree. Neither me or Henry seen that cat coming, so we both jumped.

"You crazy old thing." I reached down to pick him up, but

he scooted on ahead. "You's going the wrong way, cat," I told him.

Henry said, "Maybe he likes you better than hogs."

I was thinking I just been made fun of, but I couldn't help myself and laughed a big laugh.

The dang thing kept on following us, chasing a bird here and there, 'til we all three ended up at the big gate.

"You ain't allowed in here, cat," I said. "Go on home and see your hog friends." I give a push at him with my boot. He leaped at my laces. Man, animals like them laces.

Me and Henry was both laughing then. I crouched down and yelled, "Boo!" The cat took off. And just as I was standing up, the gate swung open fast, almost taking my head off.

The Mountain had a big guy tight around the neck, and the guy was struggling and snarling like a mad dog. Miles and another guard, blood smeared across them, was right behind, trying to grab ahold of flying arms and legs. The man was bleeding from his hand and his nose. They was all headed for the Hole, that's for sure.

Back when I first got to the penitentiary, I thought I'd like to see what was in the Hole. I sure wouldn't want to after that guy been down there a few days.

Me and Henry went on into the yard. First thing me and him seen inside the gate was a trail of bright red blood drops on the dried-up ground. And then there came two more guards out of the cellblock, and they was carrying a wood door laid out flat with somebody on it. White Beard was right there with 'em, step for step, looking real worried. The man carried on the door was Mr. Nance. I knew it was Mr. Nance just 'cause I knew him, but some others wouldn'ta recognized his bloodied, mashed-up face. He didn't see me. In fact, he maybe didn't see nothing.

"Mr. Nance!" I yelled for him, but them guards kept on moving fast past us.

Henry grabbed my crooked arm and pulled me hard toward the block. I watched over my shoulder at Mr. Nance, flat out on that door, heading into the Warden's Building.

TWELVE

I couldn't eat my food after I seen that. I thought I didn't much care for reading, but it seems I did after all. And Mr. Nance was always real patient with me.

All us men had to stay inside for most of the afternoon, 'til everybody was questioned 'bout the incident. But later we was allowed out for our required ninety minutes. Mr. Shin and Mr. Wu walked with me. Mr. Wu carried the Chinese banjo. The blood spots was gone, with dried-up puddles in their place from where somebody had threw water around.

"Jake," said Mr. Shin, "you probably want know about Mr. Nance."

"What happened, Mr. Shin? He didn't look good, not at all." We was walking across the yard, the day still hot as all get-out.

"Bad man and Mr. Nance come back from work same time.

Walk in cellblock. Bad man say mean things to Mr. Nance. Mr. Nance not say anything. I see bad man jump on him and start hitting. Mr. Nance no hit back. His face hurt floor. Got many hits before guards get to him. Happen very fast."

I was thinking out loud. "Do crazy men come in here or do men go crazy once they's here?"

Mr. Shin answered me. "Some both, Jake."

We three men walked to the far end of the yard and set down in the shade of the fence. Mr. Wu turned the pegs on the instrument, tuning up the strings.

Mr. Shin asked, "You learn to read, Jake?"

"Well, I for sure know my letters, and I can read a few things. How 'bout you? Can you read English?"

He nodded. "But not good like Mr. Nance. I read some. I teach Mr. Wu. He know some English letters now."

I asked, "Do you think Mr. Nance is gonna be all right?"

"We wait and see," said Mr. Shin. And then he asked, "You want learn to play banjo, Jake?"

Mr. Wu set the instrument in my lap, its long skinny neck sticking way out past my shoulder. He showed me how to put my fingers on a string and then pluck. The note made me laugh, but it sounded kinda lonesome, too.

The men who usually played cards wasn't playing. And the ones usually pitching quoits wasn't pitching. I think we was all thinking 'bout Mr. Nance.

I handed the instrument to Mr. Shin, and he played a slow piece of Chinese music. All the men listened. The notes floated up into the hills.

"Can't y'all play something with a tune?" yelled one of the men. Some of the others told the man to keep quiet. But Mr. Shin got up and took the banjo with him. He talked to a guard, and then the two of them headed back into the block. Didn't want no more trouble in that one day, I suppose.

Mr. Wu never said much, so him and me just kept setting in the shade, trying not to melt. Card game started up, and then some of the guys gathered up the quoits and started pitching.

I seen Mr. Shin coming back. He was carrying a piece of paper in one hand and the banjo in the other one. I could see the men was watching him walk on over and join me and Mr. Wu.

"Maybe now time to play America song."

He tuned up the strings, plucking and picking at them. He handed the piece of paper to me, and I seen right away I knew some words, or at least some letters. "Doo dah," I said out loud. "What is this, Mr. Shin?"

"Words to song," he said.

And then he picked a simple tune that even I knew, called "Camptown Races." The men all gathered round, and we sounded right good singing:

The Camptown ladies sing this song,
Doo-dah, Doo-dah
The Camptown racetrack's five miles long,
Oh! Doo-dah day.

I come down there with my hat caved in,
Doo-dah, Doo-dah
I'll go back home with a pocket full of tin,
Oh! Doo-dah day!

Going to run all night.
Going to run all day.
I'll bet my money on the bobtail nag,
Somebody bet on the bay.

Mr. Shin played the tunes for "Oh! Susanna" and then "Yankee Doodle Dandy," and the men just made up the words. They got to dancing, too. And then Mr. Shin just did some picking, sounding half American and half Chinese.

'Fore I knew it, we was all back on the block. 'Cept Mr. Nance.

THIRTEEN

September 2, 1885

White Beard come to visit 'fore I was hardly awake. Henry let him in.

"Jake," he said, setting down next to me, "have you been keeping up with your reading?"

I used my knuckles to wipe the sleep from my eyes. "Well, I got the primer here." I dug it out and showed it to him. "Henry brung it to me after Mr. Nance got hurt." What I didn't tell him was that I had not opened the book even one time since.

White Beard cleared his throat. "Yes, well, Jake. I have some news for you about Brother Nance."

"I hear stuff," I said. "I know he cain't see no more."

"That's right, Jake. We've had a doctor caring for him in the Warden's Building, but I'm afraid there's nothing more we can do to help him. He's been pardoned by the governor. Mr. Nance is going home."

As far as I knew, he was already gone.

"He'd like to see you, Jake."

"But you said he cain't see."

"Well, now, I mean he'd like you to sit with him for a bit before he leaves. Would you do that, son?"

I pictured Mr. Nance's face with no eyes. "How does he look?"

"He has a beard again. And his face is mostly healed. Will you do it?"

I knew that I would, right when he first asked, no matter what Mr. Nance looked like.

"Can we go now?" I asked.

So off we went, me and Henry and Warden White Beard. We left the block, crossed the yard, and walked on into the Warden's Building. The first door on my right stood open. I started in.

"That's not where he is, Jake," said the warden. But before I turned and walked out of that room, I seen a table and chairs. And I seen a wire coming through a hole in the outside wall and hooked up to bells.

I stepped back into the hall, and Henry closed the door. We kept on and walked up a set of steps. "Here he is, Jake."

And there was Mr. Nance, setting up in a real bed, his hands together in prayer. His beard was sorta growed back, kinda mixed-up black and white. His eyes was closed, and the one looked cockeyed and crooked where it come close to his nose. But the rest of his face just looked like a kindly old-man face.

"Is that you, Jake?" he asked.

I shouted, "Yes, sir."

Mr. Nance laughed. "I can't see you, Jake, but I can still hear you."

I felt kinda stupid. "Well, sure," I said.

"Come on and sit here." He reached out to touch a chair beside his bed. I set down. Henry and White Beard stepped outside the room and half closed the door.

"I understand that you have possession of the primer."

"Yes, sir, I do." We set quiet for a minute. "I ain't opened it since . . . "

Mr. Nance sighed. "I thought as much."

"It's not that I don't like readin', Mr. Nance. I just don't like readin' without you."

His mouth kinda tightened up. "You can do it without me, Jake. You just need a new teacher." He adjusted hisself against his pillow. "I was likely going to leave this place before you anyway. I should have let you know that."

Had a bad feeling in my gut. Then it hit me that the only other man interested in teaching reading was Mr. Hawkes. "Not Mr. Hawkes. Please not him."

"Brother Hawkes is a good man, Jake."

"Not like you. He's got a mean old face."

We set quiet again. I traced a circle on the floor with my boot.

"You were making progress. And Jake, it's so important to learn to read proper."

Before I had a chance to think, words just rushed outta me. "Mr. Shin can read some."

I heard shuffling sounds from Henry and White Beard outside the door.

Mr. Nance said, "I don't know if Mr. Shin knows any more than you do, Jake."

"Oh, he does. He can read way more words than me," I lied. But then I added, "He's real smart. He learned to play American songs on a Chinese banjo."

"Well, now, that's something," said Mr. Nance.

We both set quiet again, a big old clock ticking away on the wall.

"Would you do me a favor, Jake?"

I knew what he was gonna ask.

"Try to work with Brother Hawkes. He's a good man and a good reader. Will you do that for me, Jake?"

I nodded my head, but then I remembered he couldn't see that. "Okay, Mr. Nance. I'll try him. I really will, 'cause you want me to." Then I faced to the door with them ears hiding behind and said real loud, "But if it don't work out, me and Mr. Shin can work together."

White Beard come on in the room. He said, "You'll have to give it a real try with Brother Hawkes, Jake."

"I will. I promise." I was turned such a way as nobody could see my fingers twisted behind my back.

FOURTEEN

September 24, 1885

Mr. Nance was gone.

I give it my best shot, reading with Mr. Hawkes. That first day, I went on in there all set to learn me some new words.

"What we gonna learn today, Mr. Hawkes?" I asked.

"You do not talk unless you're addressed, Jake. Do you understand what that means?"

I stood looking.

He said, "I just addressed you, so you may answer."

"Oh." I couldn't get my eyes to look anywhere solid. "What was the question?"

This time, he did the looking around, in a mad sorta way. "Do you understand that you will not speak unless I ask you a question?"

"Oh. Yes, sir."

And that was 'bout as good as it got. He opened a book he called a hymn book. It had lines and musical notes with words underneath. He asked me what I could read. I seen some words I knew, but I told him, "It's just a buncha letters, sir. I cain't read no words."

He sighed so big I thought all his air was gone outta him. But I was wrong, 'cause he talked up a big storm: "This here is this word and that there is that word and you put them together and you got word word." Made my head hurt.

Every day, I kept going on over there, putting on a good show of trying to learn something. I made sure I was polite when I answered his questions with a string of words that didn't make no sense. He give up after ten days, and that was that.

* * *

Me and Charles kept at each other every chance we got, but never loud or mean enough to get in trouble again. Had us a pissing contest the one day. I woulda won, but the wind changed.

One time I was waiting around for Henry, and Charles was just plain waiting around. I had to ask, "So it don't much seem like you want to go to school."

"What would you know about school?"

"Well, had me my own version of school, I guess." And then I told him 'bout Mr. Nance and then Mr. Hawkes.

Charles thought 'bout all that for a minute. Then he said,

"Well, I'm sorry about Mr. Nance. But all you did was just reading. I have to do math and such."

Couldn't think of anything to match that, so I just said, "I have to sleep in a cage."

That pretty much shut him up.

Mr. Criswell's cat kept on following me and Henry home almost every day. And every time, I'd say boo and he'd turn and run back to the hogs. Crazy cat.

One day as I was mixing up a batch of slop, the cat slithered on by. "That old scrawny tomcat got a name, Mr. Criswell?"

"Nope," he said. "Just call it Cat. Been living around here for years."

"Don't suppose you know he follows me home most days."

He was mixing up his own slop recipe. "You don't say."

"What you suppose that cat wants, Mr. Criswell?"

I was used to looking at the top of his head by then. Right then he looked to me at first like he was thinking. But he took so long, I wondered if he hadn't gone to sleep standing up.

I said, "Why's that cat follow me, do ya think?"

"Well, Jake, maybe it just likes to look at new places."

Made sense to me. I liked looking at new places, mostly.

When Henry showed up, Mr. Criswell sent me to fetch something while they did some talking. On that walk home, I asked Henry, "What was you and Mr. Criswell talking 'bout?"

"Nothing important, Jake."

And then he changed the subject to one I was hoping for.

He said, "Warden Johnson has decided that you can work with Mr. Shin on your reading."

"Is that right?"

"But the warden will test both of you in two weeks and see if you're making progress."

Me and Mr. Shin would have to work real hard. No way I was gonna get pushed back on Mr. Hawkes.

Right after dinner, Henry come and led me over to Mr. Shin's cell.

"We got to work fast, Mr. Shin. If I don't read good in two weeks, Warden White Beard is gonna fire you."

Mr. Shin had his hand over his mouth, but I could see his eyes laughing.

"What?"

"Jake, you have funny words."

Being all business, I said, "Well, if we don't get a move on, I won't have no new ones."

I handed my primer over to Mr. Shin. He took a good long time looking it over. Seeing as there weren't much light to read by, even in the bright afternoon, I let him have it for a while.

Finally he looked up. "We start with alphabet," he said.

"I already done the alphabet," I said.

Mr. Shin said, "Show." He handed the slate and chalk my way. I did a fair job, *A* to *Z*, while Mr. Shin watched.

"Good, Jake." He opened the primer. "Now this," and he pointed to the alphabet lesson. "We start here."

> *A wise son makes a glad father,*
> *but a foolish son is the heaviness of his mother.*

Between us two—and Mr. Shin done the most—we got, "A wise son makes a glad __, but a __ son is the heavy of his __."

"It's somethin' 'bout a couple sons," I said. "But what's it mean he's heavy?"

Mr. Shin kept on staring at that line like the lost words was maybe gonna jump right in his ear.

He turned the page. "We try this."

> *Better is a little, with the fear of the Lord,*
> *than great treasure, and trouble therewith.*

We managed the first part of the sentence, up to "Lord." But them big words at the end, well forget that. And then the sentence didn't make no sense.

I took the book from his hand and flipped to a page that Mr. Nance showed me many times. "The Ten Commandments," I said. "I seen these before."

"Yes," said Mr. Shin, "I hear, too."

I read, "'Thou shalt have no more gods but me. Before no

idol bend thy knee.' You hear how that rhymes? 'Me' and 'knee,' they sound the same."

Mr. Shin nodded. "Read together." I didn't want to admit to myself that I remembered some of them words instead of reading them. But they was starting to feel like faces I seen every day. Like friends.

When Henry come back, I flipped the pages in the primer and asked, "What's these here words, Henry?"

He squinted up his eyes. "That first one's 'father,'" he said. "And that last one there is 'mother.'"

Both me and Mr. Shin said something like, "Ohh."

"That word is 'foolish,'" he said, pointing. Then he read the whole sentence and said what he thought it meant. A smart son makes his parents happy, but a foolish son is like a heavy weight on his parents. I figured then I must be one of them foolish sons, 'cause it sure seemed I was a heavy weight on my pa. So heavy that he just dropped me and took off.

I felt awful low right 'bout then. But the rest of those two weeks me and Mr. Shin kept on with that reading stuff, with a whole lot of help from Henry. And soon as a blink, it was the day of my reading test.

FIFTEEN

October 18, 1885

Maybe Henry was teaching me and Mr. Shin more than we was teaching each other. So what. We was all learning and filling up our days.

After dinner me and Mr. Shin, with Henry in the lead, stepped out into a cloudy afternoon and crossed on over to Warden White Beard's office. Mr. Norton seen us coming down the hall and knocked on the warden's door.

"Gentlemen," said the warden as we walked in.

I was carrying my primer, and Mr. Shin had the slate and chalk.

"Jake," said White Beard, "I'd like to see you write the alphabet."

I took the slate and chalk and started writing. I had to spit on my shirttail and erase some here and there, but I done a right nice job. "Here you go," I said, handing it across the desk.

The warden nodded and then handed the slate to Mr. Shin.

"Shin Han, do you write also or just read?"

"I write letters," said Mr. Shin. And he did. His looked more like birds and pretty things than letters. He handed the slate to White Beard, who nodded again.

"You have your primer, Jake?" he asked. And then me and Mr. Shin read what we could while White Beard tugged at that beard. And then we was done. I sure hoped it was enough.

"It looks like you're both benefiting from your reading time, Jake. So we'll just let that continue."

I 'bout grabbed him around the neck and give him a hug. Instead I said, "Yes, sir." But my ears tugged the corners of my mouth into a big old grin.

White Beard said, "I understand there's a cat that sometimes follows you from the hog pen, Jake. Is that right?"

"Sometimes."

"Well, Mr. Criswell and I discussed it, and he said next time that cat wants to make this place its home, it can stay."

I couldn't hardly believe what I was hearing.

"It's good to have a mouser around," he said. "It'll live in the yard. You just make sure it stays out of trouble, Jake."

And by then my face was almost stretched in two. "It won't be no trouble, Warden, I promise."

"Well, that's fine." He turned to Henry. "Now I'd like a

word with Jake alone, Henry. You and Shin Han, please wait in the hall."

Mr. Norton musta been glued to the door, 'cause it opened right that second and they all went out.

I figured things was going too good. Musta been time for a licking of some kind.

"You're going to have a visitor, Jake."

"A visitor?"

"A lawyer."

I didn't know if that was a good thing or a bad thing. I guessed bad, 'cause of my do-nothing lawyer at the trial.

"He's a representative of the governor, and he'll be checking on your well-being."

I said, "I'm bein' pretty well, sir, seein' as I get that dinner every day, and I get out to work the hogs. And now I'm gonna have my own cat."

"And you're learning to read."

"And that, too."

He said, "It could be a couple of weeks before he visits. I just thought you would want to know."

"Yes, sir," I said, since there weren't nothing I could do 'bout it one way or the other. Besides, maybe it wouldn't be a bad thing after all.

* * *

Just before lights-out, I was laying awake but with my eyes closed. I took a visit to my secret room. First of all, I decided

I'd let Charles out. But the Mouth, I left him locked away to rot. I said howdy to Emma, and she give me a squeal. I told her I was gonna have myself a visitor. And then I decided that while I was waiting for the real cat to come to live in the yard, I'd have that cat in there, too. Cat, this is Emma; Emma, this is Cat. And they snugged up tight together and went right off to sleep. And so did I.

It was the pistol shot that woke me up. And then the yelling and snarling, like human dogs fighting.

"Hit him!"

That was Miles, the big say-nothing guard, trying to yell but sounding like he was being strangled.

WHUMP.

Something hard hit some body part. By the light of the one burning oil lamp, I seen a pistol skip across the floor like somebody kicked it that way.

"Pull the wire!" Miles yelled in a strangled voice.

I could just see Len grabbing the knob that pulled the wire. Them bells I seen would be ringing in the other building. I 'spected the other guards was already on their way.

I heard more whumping and some whimpering, and then the door of the block flew open and all the guards who weren't on duty was in there in a hurry. By then every man was up and hollering.

"What's goin' on?"

"Mac tried to escape!"

"He's all beat up!"

"Who got shot?"

"Nobody. The shot done missed!"

Harry Smithers and Mr. Corbin was next door to me now. They didn't talk to me, but I had to ask somebody. I called over, "Mr. Smithers, you seen anything?"

"Seems that Mac thought he'd leave here tonight. Musta jumped Miles after using the clean-up cell."

I asked, "Did you see him?"

"Nah. I cain't see any more than you can. I knew somethin' was up. Mac ain't too brainy. He was throwin' out hints all day."

Mac was long gone by then. A couple of the guards was yelling for quiet, and the men settled back down. Me, I decided I'd sleep in my secret room that night, right between Emma and Cat.

SIXTEEN

November 5, 1885

I had me that visitor that Warden White Beard warned me 'bout. Mr. Bradshaw. Esquire. A lawyer.

Henry took me on over to the Warden's Building for the big meeting. We walked into a room that I hadn't never been in before. It held only a table and two chairs, one on either side. The room had a window in the wall, looking into a room next door.

A man was setting in one of the chairs, wiping at his nose with a handkerchief. "Jake, I'm Mr. Bradshaw. From the governor's office." He stood up and stuck out his hand. I didn't have no choice, so I stuck mine out and we shook. Next to my hand, his looked white like them sandstone walls. His suit was too big and hung on him like a sack.

He said, "You can sit down now, Jake." So I did. Then Mr.

Bradshaw turned and looked straight at Henry, and Henry backed on outta the room and closed the door. The window was behind me so I couldn't see if anybody was watching us or not. I pretended a sneeze and spun around enough to see White Beard and then Henry just walking into the other room.

"So, Jake. I'm here to inform you that your father has signed some papers." He dug around in a satchel on the floor by his feet.

"You seen Pa?"

He wiped that nose again. "Yes, I met with him last week."

"He coming round to see me?"

Mr. Bradshaw wouldn't look me in the eye. "I don't think so, Jake."

"That's what I figured. Did he say anything 'bout me being foolish?"

"Foolish?" He was sorting and resorting papers on the table. "Well, no, I don't think he said anything like that." And then he pulled out one particular piece of paper and turned it to face me. It was a real official-looking document. I read my name and I read Pa's name.

"What is this?" I strained to read some other words, anything.

Dang if he didn't wipe that nose again.

"Why don't you just stuff that handkerchief on up there," I said. That got him to look at me. He didn't look mean. He looked kinda tired and worn-out like.

He said, "Your father has given up his rights as a parent, Jake."

Given up his rights as a parent. "Then whose son am I?" I asked.

He looked past me, like he was hoping for some help from the other room. "Well, now, I think you know that the governor's office already sees to it that you get your meals. And when you're released, you'll be placed with a foster family."

My head was so confused. "I'll have to change my name to Foster?"

Mr. Bradshaw almost laughed. "I know this is all new. I'll try to explain it."

So he did. I didn't have a pa no more. Not Pa, not the governor. But the governor would make sure I was okay and that I got to keep eating and having a place to stay. And when I got out, I'd go live with some family the governor picked for me to live with. Didn't know why they'd want to do that, take in a kid who's been in prison.

He set the legal document on his stack of papers. When he went to pick it all up, a letter slipped out of the stack. A letter with scratchy writing on it. He glanced at it, then he tucked it with the rest of the papers into his bag. He said, "Your pa thought it was best for you, seeing as he didn't know if he could feed you once you got out."

Made sense, seeing as he never much fed me before.

"That everything?" I asked.

"Well, yes, unless you have any more questions."

"Seems I'm better off not askin'," I said. But then I did have a question. "You met the governor?"

He started to wipe that nose again but set his handkerchief on the table and just sniffled. "Well, no. I just follow orders."

"How come he let them send me here at all? They said I had to know between good and evil when I shot that pistol. But I don't even know I shot it. I don't remember nothin' but the sound of the gun goin' off."

Mr. Bradshaw looked straight at me like he seen a ghost. I didn't care how sick he was. I didn't care if I shouldn'ta asked a question like that.

"You got a answer to that?" I asked.

He shook his head. "I'm just . . . I don't know, Jake."

"Well then, I reckon I'm done." I stood up. Henry come in just then. Mr. Bradshaw stood up slowly and looked emptied out.

Walking back to the block, I told myself maybe it was best anyways, 'cause I read some words on that letter. I read the words "bad father." And maybe that was right. So maybe I'd be better off without no pa at all.

Next day I forgot all 'bout that anyways. I had myself a cat.

It seemed like Cat most liked to follow me when I weren't paying him no attention. So me and Henry was walking along. I whispered, "Cat's with us." Henry started to turn around. I whispered louder, "Don't turn around!" We picked up our pace, and I shook my boots so the laces would come undone.

We was finally facing the gate. Henry unlocked it and we walked on in.

No Cat.

So I walked matter-of-fact back on out, pretended I was tying my boot but really I was making sure it was untied. Cat followed, but kinda far back. Finally me and Henry was inside the fence, and the only thing hanging out was my boot on my foot. I shook it and the laces jumped. And so did Cat. Pretty soon, we was all inside the yard.

SEVENTEEN

November 23, 1885—My eleventh birthday

Franklin Palmer, a squatty quiet old man in for some money
scheme, give me a wood pig he carved, curly tail and all, that
fit right in my hand. We men was all out in the yard. Cat, too.
He was setting on my shoulder, having decided he liked riding
as much as pouncing, when here come Mrs. Ayres with a big
old pan filled with a birthday cake. Everybody gathered round,
and Mr. Wu had his banjo and Slim had his mouth organ, and
they all played and everybody sung to me. That made Cat
jump down and scoot off.

And then the men kinda punched me around and lifted
me up on their shoulders, laughing.

"All growed up there, Jake."

"You's taller today."

"Big man now."

Henry was there, too. "You don't have to work the hogs tomorrow, Jake."

"What for?" I asked.

"'Cause it's your birthday, I guess. They just told me you aren't going over tomorrow."

Then I heard why.

"I'm working the hogs for ya tomorrow, Jake," said Mr. McDonough, a inmate who come from the country of Scotland. "Butchering day, do ya know."

"But why ain't I goin'? That's my place."

"Well," said Mr. McDonough, "Mr. Criswell there said it wouldn't do ya good ta see what ya'd see there."

"I know them hogs better'n you ever will," I said. "And I'm goin'."

Henry shook his head. "The warden said not to take you. I've got to follow his orders."

I said, "I want to see the warden."

"Jake," said Henry, "I can't just take you over to see him whenever you want to."

I had to go to the hog butchering. It was my job. "Well, then, I want to see the governor."

Henry's pale eyebrows near 'bout jumped off his face. "Now, Jake. What's so important?"

"I got me a job, and I intend to do that job."

Henry said, "Mr. Criswell says you've been doing a fine job, Jake. And you'll go back day after."

I weren't taking the day off, but I didn't know exactly how I was gonna do that. But then Henry helped me out. He musta walked on over to see the warden at some point later in the afternoon, 'cause the next morning at breakfast he said, "You're gonna help out over at the Warden's Building this morning, Jake."

"Doin' what?" I asked.

"Don't rightly know," said Henry. "But that's the warden's orders. Let's go."

Right after me and Henry stepped out of the block into a cool-aired morning, I seen a group of men heading out the gate. I didn't have more than a second to get my plan lined up in my head. As me and Henry walked across the yard, I hit on a subject that always got Henry riled up. "How's that tooth?"

He started right in, his hands flying. "That barber didn't know what he was doing," he said. He glared out to the hills, stomping along and holding on to that bad side of his face, shaking his head and getting burned up all over again. I slipped out the gate with the men. And I reckon by the time Henry realized I weren't walking with him no more, I was halfway to Mr. Criswell's place.

I started out running fast as I could but had to slow down when my breathing was tough. And then I heard Henry coming behind. "Jake! You can't run, Jake, you'll get yourself in trouble."

The hogs was up ahead.

"And you'll get me in trouble, too, Jake."

I didn't think 'bout that part, but I wasn't turning back. I flew past the hog pen and around the shed, with Henry not ten steps behind me.

I stopped dead. And then everything I seen was real clear.

There stood Egg, his tiny soft eyes looking up at Mr. Criswell. Mr. McDonough threw a rope around Egg's snout and held him tight in place. The pistol in Mr. Criswell's hand pointed right between Egg's eyes, and then, *pop*. Almost before Egg hit the ground, dead, Mr. Criswell and Mr. McDonough was lifting up that hog. And I seen the steam coming off the tub of water over red hot coals.

And then Mr. Criswell seen me. His face didn't change, but his eyes said a whole bunch of things. *Why you here? What did you see? You'll be punished. You already been punished.*

I understood then why Mr. Criswell did not want me at that butchering. But I seen it all anyways. I stepped ahead to where the scalding process was happening. I would not run away.

I done everything he told me to do that day. Got myself burned by some hot water but ignored that. Learned 'bout cutting. Learned sausage making. Learned 'bout cleaning up. Learned my job.

Henry had run on back as soon as he seen I was working. Got myself three days of bread and water. I didn't care.

EIGHTEEN

The men stopped poking fun at me after that. Got me a head nod now and then once they all heard I could take it.

Charles come around the next week.

"Heard you helped butcher," he said, leaning on his rake.

I thought about the shiny sharp knives laid out in a row.

"I done it, I guess."

"Pa said I had a couple of years before I could help with that. How come you got to help?"

So I told him the whole story. He laughed when I told him how I set up Henry and then run like hell. He stayed mighty quiet when I told him 'bout my three days of bread and water. And then he got kinda misty-eyed when I talked 'bout Egg. Or maybe that was me.

We raked some, mostly just looking busy. Then Charles said, "Pa's bent over 'cause of me. It was my fault."

I kept working, but I was all ears.

"Pa brought home a horse named Hatty. Mean thing, I thought. But he said she was a good price, and she wasn't mean as long as you didn't sneak up on her right side."

Charles looked straight at me. "She was blind in her right eye," he said, pointing at his own.

I nodded.

"Well, I forgot all about that bad eye." He hung his head. "I come runnin' outside when Pa rode up not two weeks later. Grandad was ailin' and I wanted to tell Pa. But I ran at that right side as I was shouting, and Hatty reared back and threw Pa straight to the ground."

I didn't say nothing, partly 'cause I didn't know what to say but mostly 'cause I'd seen something Charles didn't. While Charles was spilling his whole story, Mr. Criswell come out from around the barn, and there he stood, close enough to hear every word.

"Now, Charles," said Mr. Criswell.

Charles's mouth snapped shut.

"I didn't have a good grip on that horse, Charles, so if anybody's at fault, it would be me."

Charles turned around, a couple of tears leaking out from the corners of both eyes. "Pa, you looked like you were dead."

"But I wasn't. And here I am. And so I walk a little hunched over, and I kinda nod when I laugh. Nothing I can do about that. Now go get that bucket of molasses from the barn and treat these tired old hogs."

Charles run off, and when he come back with the bucket, them tears was all dried up or wiped away. He handed the bucket to his pa and then kinda leaned into him real quick, and Mr. Criswell put an arm around his shoulder and give him a big old squeeze.

We all three pretended we was busy again, but there weren't much left to do. It felt in the air like we was all waiting for something. And then I knew. After a big breath in and out, I said, "I reckon it's my turn for confessin'."

Mr. Criswell said, "Jake, your situation is really none of our business."

"Well, I guess I'd like to tell anyways. Feel like I owe it to y'all."

And then I'm thinking that I ain't thought 'bout the shooting since the trial. I'm not sure I ever really thought through the whole thing at all.

"It was Mr. Bennett got shot. And he died." I felt a tight pull in my gut, seeing Mr. Bennett lying there in my mind. "They say I pulled the trigger, and maybe they's right. But thinking back, I don't much know how it happened."

In a real quiet voice, Charles asked, "Who was Mr. Bennett?"

So I started at the start.

NINETEEN

"Me and Pa didn't have no work right then. We was kinda drifting around Soda Springs. And then Pa remembered he had a cousin Calvin, removed a few times, who lived in them parts. Thought maybe he could find him hanging around the Whittier Saloon."

"Rough place," said Mr. Criswell, shaking his head.

"Well, we found the place and wandered on in. Pa had a couple of whiskeys. He asked the men if they knew cousin Calvin. None of the card-playing guys heard of him. And none of the pool-playing guys heard neither. Pa had a few more whiskeys, and by then he's pretty much falling down and slobbering. He starts slinging words at a guy who just come in. That was Mr. Bennett."

Charles took a step closer.

I went on. "This here Mr. Bennett owned the place. 'I don't like your type,' he says. So we's leaving. But then I see Mr.

Bennett is 'bout tipping over, hisself. He's had a few whiskeys, too. Mr. Bennett shoves Pa, hard. 'Get on out,' he says. But see, we's already getting out. Pa didn't answer back smart or nothing, and we was heading for the door. Mr. Bennett shoved Pa again, and Pa fell down. Next thing, Mr. Bennett was reaching for something, yelling, 'I'll kill you, you sorry excuse for a human being!' And then, *pop*, Pa's pistol went off. And I guess somehow it was me made it happen."

My mouth was getting dry. I licked my lips and kept going.

"Mr. Bennett grabbed at hisself sorta under his arm, and I seen blood oozin' out. Then he dropped to the ground. I'm just standing there, stuck. I ain't never seen a man bleed like that. Somebody was shouting, 'I done it, I shot him!' but I don't know who that was, 'cause it sounded like me but it weren't me. I mean I didn't know what was going on."

The three of us just stood still. Then I had to finish up telling the whole story.

"They took me and Pa to the jail, accused us both. But Pa said he didn't do it, and one man was looking right at Pa when the shot went off anyways. So Pa got dropped off the jail list."

Mr. Criswell was just leaning back, staring at me with them blue eyes, looking kinda sad.

I finished up. "Something in me musta known Mr. Bennett was going for his own gun."

Mr. Criswell asked me, "Didn't the judge hear what happened, son?"

"Well, there was a judge and there was a jury of men. When the lawyer asked did I mean to shoot Mr. Bennett, I told him what I thought I was supposed to say. I said, 'Yes, sir.' But that was all the words he let me say."

I stopped talking then, my head feeling kinda dizzy.

"You sit down here for a minute, Jake," said Mr. Criswell. He went and fetched me a dipper of water, and I gulped it down.

"I think my hand just knew that I had to shoot him, Mr. Criswell, or he woulda shot my pa."

Then Mr. Criswell was nodding, but it was a on-purpose nod. "Did you have a lawyer, Jake?"

"Yeah, but he didn't say nothing to the judge. Told me it was the first time he ever did any real lawyering."

Mr. Criswell took a dipper of water for hisself.

"They knew how old you were," he said, shaking his head.

"Yes, sir," I said. "The jury had to decide did I know good from evil when I shot that gun. The judge said it didn't make no difference 'bout my age. My lawyer thought they was gonna convict me, so he told me to plead guilty. Manslaughter. Better than murder, he said."

We three just kinda stood and breathed for a minute.

Finally Charles asked, "You ever shoot a gun before that?"

"Well, sure, but not at anything living. I don't like hurting things, even when they's food."

Mr. Criswell give me a pat on my back. Charles handed me my rake.

Then we went ahead at our work, and that pig pen weren't never that clean before or again.

Later, me and Charles was roughhousing some, being done with our work and me just waiting for Henry. I jumped on a fence rail to show Charles the way Cat pounced. A board let go, and a sticking-out nail cut right through my trousers and across my leg just above my knee. Blood shot out and then seeped on down my pant leg. It looked like it musta been somebody else's leg standing there bleeding, but then the burning pain started.

Charles run and grabbed my shirt hanging in the shed. He quick wrapped it around my leg above the cut and pulled it into a tight knot.

"Get on," Charles said, and I climbed onto his back. He took off fast as he could to find his pa. My mouth was so dry, and I was trying to think of anything but my leg. I rode past a garden, potatoes, sugar beets, fat yellow sunflowers at the end of each row, soaked up with sun, staring at me with their big seed faces.

I kept thinking, *Not my leg! Not my leg!* Then I seen a white house and a lady on the porch. She shouted, "Charles! What happened?"

She run over to us, and Charles dropped me to the ground.

"A nail did it," he said, and untied the blood-soaked shirt. The cut weren't as big as it felt, and it had quit seeping. But most of my whole pant leg was red.

"Margaret, get a wet cloth."

Who was Margaret? And then I caught a glimpse. Light brown dress, blue ribbon tied at the bottom of a darker brown braid, taller than Charles but not much. And not ugly like Charles. Not at all. She was gone, into the house. And then I started seeing double.

"I need water," I said. "I'm seeing two of things."

Margaret was back on the porch with a wet cloth that she handed to her ma. Margaret heard me and laughed right out loud. "You're not seeing double. They are double. They're twins." Her ma wiped at my cut.

"Ouch! I'll do it," I said, looking back and forth at the twins.

Margaret said, "Lily and Annie, meet Jake."

"We're five," said Lily or Annie.

"Margaret is ford-teen," said the other one.

"How old are you?" asked the first one.

"Inside, girls," said Mrs. Criswell.

The twins stood looking for a second, then the first one said, "This is more fun than inside."

Mrs. Criswell and Margaret laughed. And then here come Mr. Criswell carrying a tiny little baby, its arms waving at me or maybe at the sky. The two stopped right in front of me. "Jake. I thought I could trust you."

"I'll fix the fence."

"Yes, you will," he said, rocking that baby side to side. "Seems you've met everyone else. This here is Emma."

Well, I woulda fell over 'cept I was already on the ground.

"I like that name Emma," I said.

"It's a good name," said Mr. Criswell. He looked through the rip in my trousers at my cleaned-off leg. "Rusty nail or clean?"

"Clean," I told him.

"Needs a stitch or two, Leandra, don't you think?"

"What? No. It's fine," I said. I stood up quick. "I gotta go fix that fence board."

* * *

Charles stood watching while I pounded a nail into a new place on that rail. "Nice and solid," I said. Then I couldn't help myself. "You got a whole mess of sisters."

"Yeah, so what," said Charles. "You're gonna have an ugly scar on that leg, and you've already got a face to match it."

I tossed some straw his way, but mostly I just laughed.

My leg healed up nice in 'bout a week. Left just enough scar to look tough.

Another batch of piggies come to be a few weeks later. Nine of them that time, and we didn't lose a one, even with the cooler weather. They come in the middle of the night again. Somebody ought to tell them sows about time.

Charles was there, too. "That one isn't moving, Pa."

One of the piggies was still. Mr. Criswell said, "Rub it with this rag, Jake. Help get it going."

So I picked it up and rubbed and rubbed, and that piggy

started squirming. "He's trying to get away already."

"Well, sure he is," said Charles. "He needs his mama. Unless you've got some milk coming out of you somewhere." We all laughed.

Got to have my breakfast with the Criswells that morning. Mrs. Criswell didn't make anything like that slop I usually ate. We had us corn bread and bacon and eggs and milk right from a cow.

"Are you my brother?" asked Lily or Annie.

Mrs. Criswell said, "Now, Annie, you know Jake is just a guest."

It felt right nice to be a brother, even if it only lasted for a second.

TWENTY

December 19, 1885

We men was in the yard like usual, moving around to stay warm as the day was right crisp. Me and Cat played chase or pounce, or he just set on my shoulder.

Christmas was coming up, but with no presents coming with it, it didn't seem much more than another nice big meal to look forward to. Good enough for me.

When the bad time started, I was standing near the last piece of wood fence. Me and Cat, with him setting on my shoulder, was talking 'bout nothing in particular when I seen a shadow moving over me. I turned quick.

"Move it." John Harrow, a man in for robbing a train, threw a loud whisper my way.

"What you say?"

"Shut up, you stupid kid. You and your cat. Move it."

"We ain't doin' nothin'," I said. And then I seen him look on over toward Martin Winn, a man in for beating a guy so bad the guy didn't never walk right again.

John Harrow showed a stick of dynamite inside his shirt, and I knew. He bared his teeth and growled at me.

My legs wouldn't work, but my mouth did. "Henry!"

Before I knew anything else, John Harrow grabbed Cat from my neck. Cat tried to dig in but didn't hardly get a scratch at me, he was grabbed so quick. Then John Harrow threw Cat right at the stone wall. *Crack.* Cat laid in a heap.

"That's what you get for your big mouth, kid." A pistol in Harrow's hand pointed my way.

Henry come running over with his Winchester at his shoulder, yelling, "Pull the wire!" Miles run and pulled at the wire. It come slipping out of the wall, cut in two. The guards inside wasn't gonna help us.

I was too angry to care. I went for John Harrow like I was a wild animal, jumped on him, scraping at his eyes and clawing at anything on him I could reach. Harrow got his knee on my chest, pinning me to the ground.

Martin come running and grabbed the dynamite stick, stuffing it in at the base of the wood fence. "We're gettin' out!" he yelled. And then he pulled a pistol outta his shirt, waving it back and forth at Henry and Miles. The other men in the yard was hanging way back or trying to hide, but no more guards was coming. I scraped Harrow's face, broke free, and took off for the Warden's Building. Harrow took a shot, but I kept running. I grabbed off my boot and threw it at the window. The glass behind the bars shattered. In a few seconds the door swung open.

"What the . . . ?" Len run out and seen what was going on. He shouted inside to the other guards, who come charging out, armed with everything they had.

I run back to Cat. He was laying there in a heap. I fell on my knees and covered over him.

The guards was all out. Everybody was shouting, guns drawn, shots fired in the air. John Harrow bent down at the wall, trying to light the fuse on the dynamite. He didn't see me coming. I run fast like a train on a track right at him and knocked him over. We rolled around and over, and I hit him with my fist and kicked at him. He pounded me on the side of my head with his pistol.

BOOM! The dynamite exploded, sending wood pieces over John Harrow and Martin and Henry and me. My ears felt like they blew up, too, and then they filled with a hissing sound.

John Harrow stood up. "You damn kid. You ruined it." He raised his pistol. I seen it clear as day, aimed right between my eyes. Then everything slowed way down, like time was trying to stop. I watched his finger pull at the trigger. And then I seen a crazy thing. I seen some big wild thing attacking him from the side. I heard *bang!* Then everything went black.

* * *

A lantern on a table glowed low beside me. I tried setting up but fell back, my head heavy, like it was filled with rocks. But I'd seen enough to know I was laying on a white bed with white sheets surrounded by white walls. And all of a sudden I couldn't stop shaking. Felt like I was in a winter room, freezing cold. The side of my head hurt, and I couldn't grab ahold of any real thoughts.

I squeezed my eyes tight as I could. I seen stars, and then I seen things that didn't make no sense at all. There was Cat's gold face, his whiskers moving as he told me to look them sunflowers in the face. Mr. Wu's banjo played music by itself, and trays of food flew past me, smashing into stone walls. I hugged at my shoulders, shivering, calling out to Pa and to White Beard and even to Margaret. "Make it go away," I heard myself shouting. "Make it stop."

And then someone was holding on to my arms. It was Miles. I struggled against him, got my hand free, and slapped his face.

He shook me by my shoulders and held on.

His face looked all blurry to me. "Cat says it's the sunflowers," I heard myself mumbling.

Miles said, "You ain't makin' sense."

My eyes cleared some, and I spit out, "Get your hands off me!" Miles let go, and I fell onto my side.

I musta slept some, 'cause I woke wrapped and struggling in a blanket. I smelled food and for a second I thought I was back in my cage. But I was still in that white room on that white bed, a tray of beef and beans setting on a chair just inside the door.

I knew that chair and that bed. They was where I seen Mr. Nance for the last time. Him in the same bed, trying to heal. So I was supposed to be healing, too. Cat really was dead, and so was some men, I reckoned, and I was so hungry I'da ate anything. I got off the bed, steadied myself, and then picked up the tray. Didn't taste nothing, but it all went down. The shaking slowed some then.

Miles come in. He took the empty tray from me and turned to leave.

I asked, "Mr. Harrow get out?"

Miles shook his head. "Norton shot him dead."

"I thought I seen a wild animal," I said. "Musta been the Mountain instead." Miles didn't say nothing else, but I had the feeling he knew more. "What happened?" I asked.

Miles said, "Martin's in the Hole. Got a bullet in his behind."

I mighta laughed at that before, but not now. "I heard a lot of shooting. What else happened?"

"Norton," said Miles. "Jumped in front of you."

"What?" I searched through my brain, trying to remember.

"He took a bullet was meant for you."

A bullet. Meant for me.

"Is he all right?"

Miles didn't answer.

The Mountain saved me, and now he was dead. That shivering started up again. I took up that blanket, and then I crawled under the bed.

TWENTY-ONE

Next morning, Miles come and got me. I held firm to the underneath of that bed frame, but he pulled me out like I was nothing.

"You ain't sick. You gotta go back to your cell," he said, holding on to my arm, and we started down the hall. I heard moaning when we passed the next room. Miles said, "Slim got hit in the leg. Might lose it."

We got to the door leading out to the yard. I couldn't face the men. I tried to hold tight to the knob, but Miles pushed that door open and I stumbled outside. I reached to pull my shirt up over my head, but all was quiet, the men being at work, I figured.

We walked across the yard. Two men I didn't know was unloading stone from a cart, filling in temporary where the dynamite blew that last section of wood away. Miles unlocked the cellblock door. I walked in, just wanting to get on up to my cage and hide.

The men weren't out working. Every one of them was in his cell. When they seen me, they started throwing words.

"Troublemaker."

"Sissy."

"Why you here, boy?"

"Stupid kid."

"Nothin' but trouble."

"Jackass."

"Messed up their escape."

And they flicked stones and threw pieces of food and anything else they could shoot out at me through their food slots or them flat bars.

Henry was on duty, and he seen me come in but looked away. He picked up a wood club laying at his feet. He walked over and slammed it into the bars of the closest cell. That metal sound echoed off the walls, and his voice, angry like I never heard, followed along. "Next man throws something will join Martin in the Hole."

It got quiet right quick.

I followed Miles over to the stairs and up to my cage, not looking at nothing or nobody on the way. Nothing mattered. I was just heading to my cage to disappear. I would not work the hogs. I would not speak to no one. And I would not eat again.

Just after I got locked in, the guards come and got most of

the men, taking them to Mr. Norton's funeral. I heard them talking. They was burying him just outside the wall, in the cemetery where a couple of inmates was laid to rest after they was hanged. The Mountain was to have his own separate place. Nobody asked was I going.

When they was gone, I took off my boots and threw them hard as I could at the wall. Anything I could reach, which weren't much, I threw it, too. The primer, my carved wood pig. And then I walked back and forth 'til the men come back. Later, when Mrs. Ayres brung my dinner tray, I stood facing the wall 'til she walked away.

On my bunk in the middle of the night, I closed my eyes tight and tried to visit Emma one last time, but she was gone. In her place was something like the Hole. Nothing but black dirt all around. Musta fell asleep 'cause I woke like I was digging at dirt, my fingers scraping at the wall, trying to get some air. I stayed awake the rest of the night.

I heard the men leaving for breakfast. I would not join them. Miles had the keys, but I just shook my head when he come near my cell. Nobody said one word to me. Didn't see Henry. Didn't go to work. Didn't get no order to see the warden. 'Cept for a silent visit to the honey bucket, I laid on my bunk the whole day, looking at exactly nothing. When the dinner bell rang, my mouth started to water. Mrs. Ayres brung my tray, but I would not eat.

"You've gotta eat, Jake," she said. "The warden says you at

least gotta drink." She stood with that tray for maybe a whole minute, but I laid on my bunk with my back to her and she went away.

Two more days I didn't eat. Didn't know if I wanted to live.

In the night, flying creatures come to me in my dreams. It was hot like I was in a stew pot, and the birds' claws reached for me. But I had claws, too, and attacked them and scraped at feathers and skin. I lapped at their blood, more thirsty than I thought possible. And then I seen a sea of hogs. And there stood Egg looking at me, looking at a spot right between my eyes. In his pig voice, Egg said, "Didn't have no choice." And Shin Han was there, and he had a paper with song words on it, but I couldn't read them. And then Pa was there, handing me a letter. I seen that letter before. I struggled to look closer, and then my sleeping self knew where I seen that letter. The lawyer, Mr. Bradshaw. The letter with scratchy handwriting on it. It was a letter for me from Pa.

I woke in a sweat. I wanted my letter. And since I couldn't rely on nobody else for nothing, I would have to read it myself.

I felt around in the pitch dark 'til I found the primer. It was bent-up some, laying in the corner, but the pages was all still there. It was too dark to see, so I set on the edge of my bunk 'til the sun come up with just enough light to read.

My hands was shaking. What could I read for real? I tried the alphabet. The letters wouldn't stand still. I tried the page 'bout foolish sons, but I couldn't remember, and I couldn't make sense of none of it. I thought of Mr. Nance, but then I remembered Mr. Hawkes.

I heard jangling keys, and the men was rustling around, readying to go to breakfast. Got on my boots and stood at the door. Howard, usually an afternoon guard, come up the steps to unlock cells that morning. I joined the other men and headed down to breakfast. My boots felt way heavy, but I kept moving.

Henry was working breakfast. He didn't look at me, but he set a heaping bowl of slop in front of me. I shoveled it in and drank down that tin cup of water so fast I 'bout drowned. The men got up to leave. I didn't look at Henry when I said, "I'm goin' to the hogs today." I stood up, but my legs folded. Henry grabbed me under my arms before I hit the floor.

"Don't know if you can make it that far, Jake," he said.

I wobbled on out the door.

TWENTY-TWO

Took me some extra time to make it to the hogs, I felt so weak. Didn't neither one of us talk none 'til we reached the pen. Mr. Criswell seen me and started over with Charles right behind him. To Henry I said, "I'd like to see the warden sometime. I know he's busy. Just when he can."

Henry nodded. Then he turned and left me at my job.

Mr. Criswell asked, "You okay, Jake?" And Charles's face asked the same thing.

I nodded, reaching for my rake. We three worked the hogs. I had to hold on to the fence a few times, feeling sorta dizzy. Charles had a couple apples in his pockets. He give me one, and I ate the whole thing, seeds and all. Then he give me what he hadn't yet ate. And then I kept on working.

Me and Charles was getting dippers of water. I asked him, "You read much?"

He gagged on a mouthful of water. "So you remember how to talk?"

I didn't feel like fooling around. "You read?"

"Yeah, I can read. Some. Margaret's the big reader. Always correcting everybody."

We walked back to the hogs, done with the day's work. I asked, "You got a book I can use? A easy book."

"I don't know."

Mr. Criswell said, "We have some books you can borrow, Jake. I'll have Margaret pick them out."

I nodded, leaning again on the fence just as Henry come into view.

Mr. Criswell said, "Make sure you clean your plate at dinnertime, Jake. We don't want you to disappear on us."

Charles said, "See you tomorrow."

All I could manage was "Yeah." And then me and Henry started back. We wasn't silent on that trip.

We walked some, and then Henry said, "I'm not your mama, Jake." We kept moving on. "I don't know how I got to be the one to take care of you all the time."

"Didn't ask ya."

Henry picked up a rock and whipped it at the hills. "Earl Norton was a good man." He stopped walking. I did, too. "It isn't your fault that he's dead, but I can't help thinking it might have been different if you weren't here. But that isn't your fault. They should not have put you here."

We both started out again.

Henry went on. "I didn't really think about maybe getting shot when I took this job. Nobody thinks it'll happen to him. But things happen all right." He snorted some and then spit. "I did want you to know that it looks like maybe Slim won't lose his leg after all."

I nodded. "Why'd you take this job?" I asked.

"It's steady work."

"That it?"

He got quiet. Then he said, "My father never thought I was tough. I knew I was."

"So what's he say 'bout this here job?"

"He's been dead a few years now."

I had to smile, the first time in days. "So you took this job to prove that you's tough. To prove it to your pa who's dead."

Henry kicked at a clump of prairie grass.

I said, "You's too smart for this job, Henry. You can read and you can understand things other people don't get at all. You ought to be a lawyer. You's way smarter than that idiot got me stuck in here."

I was talking to the wide-open air. Henry had stopped a few steps back, and he had a sorta surprised look on his face.

He caught up to me. "I've got some money saved up now," he said, "but I didn't know what I was saving for. Maybe I should try to be a lawyer."

"That'd show your old dead pa."

We both laughed at that.

* * *

Christmas come and went with some food and some singing, but nobody much seemed to care.

The day after, heard I was finally going to see Warden Johnson. I had a lot to get off my mind.

Henry walked me on over. Mr. Davenport, the new assistant warden with his sharp pointy nose, looked over his glasses at me and Henry for a long second and then got up and led us into the warden's office.

Henry closed the door and stood beside it. I set down in the chair in front of the warden's desk.

"How have you been doing, Jake?" White Beard leaned forward at his desk.

I said, "Fine, sir."

"I didn't check on you myself these last days because I had a lot to do."

I nodded. And then I said, "I'm sorry 'bout Mr. Norton. I didn't never mean for that to happen."

The warden said, "He was just doing his job, Jake. He was going for Mr. Harrow's gun when he got shot."

That chair felt mighty uncomfortable. I shifted around.

"I understand you've been eating again," said the warden.

My head drooped down. "Yes, sir."

"Well, Jake, you asked to see me."

"There's somethin' I want."

"What's that, Jake?" he asked.

"A letter from my pa."

The warden looked on over at Henry and then back at me. "I don't think your pa is going to write, Jake."

"I seen a letter when that Mr. Bradshaw was here. He had a letter for me from Pa, but he didn't give it to me."

The warden set up straight. "Is that right?"

"I want it. And I'll read it. Myself. With no help from nobody."

"Are you reading again with Mr. Han?"

"It's Mr. Shin, sir. In China, the names is backwards to us."

"Oh. Well, then," he said, "are you reading with Mr. Shin?"

"That's part of what I wanted to tell you. I want to keep reading, but, well, I think Mr. Hawkes might be the best teacher. Actually, I think Henry would be the real best, but he's goin' on to be a lawyer."

Henry made a noise like he was 'bout to suffocate.

The warden didn't look toward Henry, but he smiled and said, "Well, that's a good thing, Jake. Henry's a smart man. We could use some smart lawyers."

Henry stood, shuffling his feet.

"I got more years in this place, so I figure I'll learn readin' good enough to read Pa's letter on my own sometime before I get out. And I think Mr. Hawkes should teach Mr. Shin and Mr. Wu, too. And anybody else wants to learn to read."

"I'll talk to Brother Hawkes about your idea."

"And I'm gettin' some books from Margaret. I mean, from Mr. Criswell."

"I see."

That chair was making my backside fall asleep. "Can I go now?"

"Yes, of course, Jake." I got up to leave. "Henry," said the warden, "you come on back after you get Jake out to the yard."

Henry's voice sounded like a scared mouse. "Yes, sir," he said. And I went on out to finish my ninety outside minutes.

TWENTY-THREE

Mr. Hawkes got awful uppity, heading up a bunch of know-nothing inmates, teaching us to read. New Year's come and went and then all of January and on into February. Had us some snowy days, and snow or not it got mighty cold, outside and in. But I didn't slack off reading. Felt I was making some progress, but I never showed Mr. Hawkes the books Margaret give to me. Weren't none of his business. And I was reading some pieces in them by myself.

Me and Mr. Shin and Mr. Wu and another man named Joe was setting at the breakfast table where we met most afternoons to read. It weren't going so good.

"What is that word?" asked Mr. Hawkes, holding up the slate. But I couldn't figure it out. I was trying to cram too many things into my thick brain. Felt like my head would explode. Mr. Hawkes said nice and loud, "Perhaps you've learned all that you will ever learn, Jake." I didn't think he was right, but the next day I panicked, just in case he was.

"I'm not supposed to tell you," said Henry as we walked quick toward the hogs, trying to stay warm in the cold morning air.

"Well, if you ain't supposed to tell me, then don't," I said.

Henry slowed down some. "You're getting out, Jake."

I stopped walking.

"They's throwin' me out?"

"They aren't throwing you out, Jake. You're getting a pardon. From the governor."

I was afraid to think 'bout what that meant.

"You've got about three weeks until the lawyer comes, Jake. Don't mention that I told you. I wasn't supposed to."

"Three weeks?" I had three weeks left to learn enough reading to 'cipher Pa's letter.

At the hogs, I shoveled double fast.

"Hold on, Jake," said Mr. Criswell. "Where's the fire?"

"I was wonderin', well, you know how to read, don't you, Mr. Criswell?"

"I do." He bent back and looked at me, grinning ear to ear. "Are you saying that you'd rather learn to read than work the hogs?"

"Yes, sir. That's right."

"Well then, finish up here, and then you come on over to the house."

He didn't tell me Margaret was going to be my teacher.

That first day, I wasn't able to hear much of anything 'cept her voice drifting around my head. I coulda ridden right out on a cloud. Soon as I left her, I realized I only had three weeks less one day left 'til I would have to read my letter or maybe never learn any more reading. Enough of that mooning stuff. The next day, I pretended Margaret was just some old dried-up schoolteacher. And mostly I just didn't look her way.

I asked, staring at the page, "Why don't this word say 'throwg' instead of 'through'?"

She said, "Doesn't."

"Doesn't what?" I really was trying.

"Why *doesn't* it say 'throwg' instead of 'through'?"

"Okay. Why *doesn't* it?"

"That's just the way it is, Jake. Some of the words, you'll just have to memorize."

I nodded. "'Til they look like old friends."

She laughed. Her chin kinda lifted up when she done that. Had to tell myself, *Old dried-up schoolteacher, old dried-up schoolteacher.*

* * *

I weren't getting anywhere that afternoon with Mr. Hawkes's reading lesson. He just plain give me the hardest words possible. Mr. Shin was having as much trouble, and Mr. Wu and Joe had done give up. So after Henry took me to the honey bucket cell before bed, I asked him, "Could you help me with the primer?" He stayed 'til there weren't no more light to read, and every day he helped as much as he had time. And by the end of my three weeks, we had got through most of it.

The next day, Henry told me, "Today's the day, Jake. You'll see the warden after dinner. Remember, you don't know anything."

"I already got you in trouble, Henry, tellin' him 'bout your lawyerin' and such. I won't let on."

"It's okay, Jake. I might not have been brave enough to tell him myself."

Had my breakfast, worked the hogs, read with Margaret, ate my dinner of dried beef with potatoes, and I was setting at the reading table, not listening to one word Mr. Hawkes said.

"Jake," said Henry, who had just come into the block.

"Yes, Henry," I said.

"The warden would like to see you."

Mr. Hawkes give me a look like *You done it now*.

"Excuse me, Mr. Hawkes." I followed Henry out the door and across to Warden Johnson's office.

TWENTY-FOUR

March 4, 1886

I set before the warden on that hard wood chair. Mr. Bradshaw, Esquire, set in a chair beside me.

"Jake," said the warden, "you remember Mr. Bradshaw?"

I crossed my arms and said, "I sure do."

"Well, Jake, Mr. Bradshaw has some good news."

Mr. Bradshaw cleared his throat. It didn't work, so he done it again. And then he said, "You've been pardoned by the governor."

"Pardoned?" I asked. "What does that mean?"

"It means you're getting out of the penitentiary."

Even though I knew it was coming, those words shook me. Didn't know if I wanted to laugh or cry.

"I have the papers here if you want to see them," he said.

"Yes, sir, I'd like to see them." My hands was wet with sweat, and they was shaking just a little bit.

Mr. Bradshaw handed them to me. "If you'd like me to read—"

"No, sir. I can read."

I seen Mr. Bradshaw look over at the warden. I sorted through the papers, some as long as my arm. But no letter.

I turned and looked straight at Mr. Bradshaw. "Where's my letter?"

"Letter? What letter?"

"My letter from Pa. The letter you was supposed to give me last time you set here."

His mouth dropped open.

Warden Johnson said, "Is there a letter, Mr. Bradshaw?"

Mr. Bradshaw shut his mouth and then reached slow down into his bag and pulled out my letter. I dropped the other papers on the desk and grabbed for it, but he held it as far away from me as he could.

"It's best you don't have this, Jake," said Mr. Bradshaw.

"It's mine. It's a letter to me, ain't that right?"

"Well, yes. But . . ."

Warden Johnson said, "Are you sure you want it, Jake?"

"Don't matter what it says. I mean, it *doesn't* matter what it says. It's mine."

Mr. Bradshaw thought for a second and then he handed the letter to me. I folded it and tucked it in my shirt. Looked like Mr. Bradshaw wanted to say something, but I ignored him and asked the warden, "The rest of this stuff, what does it say, without readin' the whole dang stack?"

I pushed the papers across the desk to Warden Johnson, who straightened them into a neat pile. "Basically, it says that even though you were sentenced to five years for the crime of manslaughter, the jury at your trial was unable to agree as to whether you were responsible for your acts or not."

"But I thought . . ."

Warden Johnson held up one particular long document in both hands and continued on. "It says you were sentenced upon a plea of 'guilty of manslaughter.' That shouldn't have happened, Jake. Your lawyer should not have had you plead guilty."

I set up a little straighter.

"It seems that some businessmen took up your cause, Jake. This is a petition they sent to the governor. It says that if you're required to serve the full term of imprisonment, it will tend to demoralize instead of reform you. I think you understand what that means." He set the document down and rested his forehead in his hands. "I believed that right from the start, but I had no choice."

"It weren't your fault," I said. "And now you's helping make it right."

The warden's old eyes got shiny, and he wiped them with his handkerchief.

I had to know. "Where are they sending me?"

He smiled then. "You're going to live with a foster family that the governor's office arranged for you, with my help."

And I knew what family that had to be. I was practically a brother already.

"That's fine," I said, jumping up from my chair.

"Don't you want the information, Jake?"

"No, sir. I'm fine." I turned to go. "Wait, when am I gettin' out?"

"Tomorrow, son."

Couldn't hardly believe it. "Okay, then. I'll be ready." I was mostly out the door when I leaned back in. "Mr. Bradshaw? Henry here is going to be a lawyer. He's real smart. You might want him to work with you."

He managed, "Oh. Well, maybe we can talk."

And then I remembered something I had to do. I looked right at Warden Johnson and said, "Thank you, sir."

I walked on out to the yard for my ninety minutes, Pa's letter resting next to my skin. I kept to myself, just kinda walking around and around. What if I had not learned enough to read what Pa wrote? I couldn't let anyone else read my letter for me. But then I thought maybe I could. Maybe I'd let my new pa, Mr. Criswell.

TWENTY-FIVE

March 5, 1886

On my way to the hogs, I said, "Henry, I don't have to eat that mornin' swill ever again."

He laughed. "That's right."

"I'll have me some eggs and milk and maybe some flapjacks even." I licked at my lips.

"Hold on there. Don't get ahead of yourself."

But I already pictured myself at the breakfast table, Annie and Lily asking a thousand questions. And Margaret. And, okay, Charles, too. I was practically running by then. We come up on the hogs. "Mornin', Mr. Criswell," I said, and I give him a right big smile.

"Morning, Jake. Seems you're chipper today." He was playing along.

"Yes, sir."

"I heard you're being released today. Is that right?"

"Heard that, huh?" I was playing along, too.

Charles come around from the shed 'bout then.

"Yep," I said, nice and loud. "I'll be moving along down the road after my dinner."

Charles stood beside me, looking at me like he didn't know.

I kept on. "Moving along to somebody's house is what they tell me."

Now Charles shifted from one foot to the other to the other.

Mr. Criswell said, "You got something to say, Charles?"

He kicked at a clump of dirt. "You coulda told me, Pa. That's all."

"Well, I didn't."

Guess Mr. Criswell wanted to keep the big old surprise all to hisself.

Charles asked, "You really leaving that place today, Jake?"

"That's right. Free like a bird."

He stood, nodding. Not like a Mr. Criswell nod, but like a trying-to-make-sense-of-it nod. "So, where ya going?"

I opened my mouth to tell Charles the big surprise, but Mr. Criswell got real busy then, giving orders. Do this, do that. Me and my new almost-brother couldn't clean nothing right, couldn't move them hogs fast enough. Didn't get to read with Margaret. And by the time Henry come back, I still had my letter tucked in my shirt, unread.

"Henry," said Mr. Criswell, "you bringing a new man starting tomorrow?"

He was really taking that surprise thing all the way.

Henry nodded. "Rufus Jensen." He was a smiley old man, a ranch hand got caught stealing. Didn't matter what name Henry said, since I was the one gonna be working the hogs anyways.

Charles got caught in the surprise. "You mean I have to keep going to school?"

Mr. Criswell said, "Looks like it, Charles."

And then without thinking, my mouth said, "Will I go to school, too, or will I just keep on working the hogs?"

Mr. Criswell leaned back and looked at me with his full face. He looked to Charles, too. And then I knew I was wrong 'bout my foster family.

I started laughing. "Hey, just making a joke. I know y'all want me to stick around, but, well, I gotta go." I started walking away.

"Hold up, Jake." Mr. Criswell come on over to me.

"Mrs. Criswell and I talked to the warden. We wanted you to stay right here with us. But the decision had already been made, Jake. We tried to fight it, but . . . "

Charles stamped the ground. "It ain't fair."

"Don't matter," I said right quick. "I can get by anywhere."

"Now don't go off mad, Jake."

I weren't mad. I was . . . well, I didn't know what I was.

Mr. Criswell put his hand on my shoulder. "We're hoping you can come visit sometime."

I leaned into him and asked kinda quiet, "You know where I'm goin'?"

"No, Jake, I don't know. Henry, you know?"

Henry said, "I'm afraid I don't. But maybe it's not far from here."

Charles come over and stuck out his hand. I shook it, but neither one of us had nothing to say.

Me and Henry walked back slow. I scuffed the path and looked up and around to the hills one last time. At the wood gate, I walked in for the last time. Nothing would be familiar from now on.

Ate my last dinner in my cage, extra bread included. Mrs. Ayres wished me luck and even shook my hand through the food slot. I packed up my stuff. Some old clothes, a couple books, a carved wood pig without a tail. Weren't much more than I come with.

And then I set on my bunk the last time and opened Pa's letter. Turned out I was fretting over nothing. I could read every single word.

Jake,

You won't never red this anywho but I've a mind to put down what I think. Your ma took sick when yous just learnin to walk. Didn't know what to do with ya when she up and died. Still didn't know what to do when you took my gun and used it on Mr. Bennett. I ain't a bad father, I didn't never want to be one so it's best you live somewheres away from me.

Got a new wife and she don't want a leftover kid, so we's goin on more west were I will work and make a new life. Don't cause no troubles to no one. Do what yous told and keep that mouth shut.

Your pa

TWENTY-SIX

It was time to go. My belly was full and my head was over-flowing.

Henry come for me. I picked up my bag and walked out and down them steps for the last time. The men was out doing their ninety minutes in the yard. I didn't have much to say to any of them but Mr. Shin and Mr. Wu.

"Thanks for playin' that nice music," I said. "And for tryin' to teach me to read."

"You a good reader and good man, Jake," said Mr. Shin. He shook my hand and give me a quick head bow.

Miles and Len shook my hand, too, and wished me good luck. And then me and Henry left through the round-top gate one last time. Behind us come Warden Johnson. We all stood outside the gate and watched a cloud of dust coming our way. A wagon pulled up hitched to two raggedy horses and driven by a skinny man wearing a washed-out red shirt and overalls and a hat looked like he set on it more than wore it. He didn't turn his head, just said, "I'm to pick up the boy."

Warden Johnson said, "Mr. Drummond, I'd like a word with you." The man stepped down to meet with the warden.

I turned to Henry and said, "Once you's a big-man lawyer, you can come on and visit me, let me know how lawyerin' is."

Henry reached out his hand, and we shook. A couple of tears run down his face, and he didn't even try to wipe them away.

The warden handed some papers to Mr. Drummond. "These are Jake's official documents, sir. We should have given them to you at the lawyer's office." He slapped Mr. Drummond on the back and left his hand there a second. "He's a good boy."

Mr. Drummond gave a quick nod. He folded them papers and tucked them inside his overalls. "Thank you kindly, Warden. Time to go, son." He stepped on up one side and I stepped on up the other side, and them horses pulled away before I barely set down.

We took off, bumping along steady and slow. Mr. Drummond didn't say nothing. I looked back at that fence, now all white stone, getting small behind me. Got kinda blurry-eyed, so I turned forward and didn't look at nothing. We kept on aways, and then we started a gradual climb.

My mouth got to thinking out loud. "You sure you want me around, Mr. Drummond?"

At first I thought he didn't hear me, but then he said, "Need some help with the livestock. Warden says you're a worker."

"Hogs?" I asked.

"Sheep," he said.

Sheep.

So they was gonna work me. Well, if I was gonna work, I had to know was I gonna eat.

"Will I get dinner every day?" I asked. "I got dinner in there every single day."

I thought I saw his chin twitch, but all he said was "You'll eat."

That's all I needed to know.

We kept on, the horses slowing even more with the climb. The air felt like it was thinking 'bout spring as the trail wound up around a hill. And then, there stood a tall crookedy house and a small slapped-together barn and some chickens and a fence full of sheep. I didn't know sheep and weren't happy 'bout that. But the critters that really shook me up stood lined up on a porch that leaned a little to one side. Them critters was girls, every darn one of them.

TWENTY-SEVEN

I counted seven girls in a row, starting 'bout my waist high and on up taller than me. The last girl weren't a girl, she was Mrs. Drummond, and she was as skinny as Mr. but with a tight, dried-up face.

"You get on to work, Jake," she said. I jumped down and followed Mr. Drummond to them stinky old sheep. With the day getting on late, mostly I learned what I'd be doing from then on. Mr. Drummond pointed some here and there, and he didn't say one word more than he had to. I figured out we was done for the day when he wiped his hands on his pant legs and started walking toward the house. I followed him up the creaky steps.

It was time for their dinner meal, my second one that day. I set at the table with them six total silent girls and Mr. and Mrs. Drummond. A small girl whispered, "He's a boy." That got all them girls to giggling. Mr. Drummond snickered, too.

133

Mrs. banged her fist on the table, and everybody hushed up. But I could still see them all grinning.

I ate what the oldest girl put down in front of me. Weren't no heap of food like I was used to, but I wouldn't starve.

"You'll do what you're told, Jake," said Mrs. "You'll work the sheep and the chickens and anything else Mr. Drummond needs. And you will go to church every Sunday and study your Bible. And you will sing with us when Mr. Drummond plays his banjo, and you will do it all without complaint."

I chewed and listened.

"And you will go to school when time affords. You will read, and you will not be ignorant."

School. Me going to school. Without thinking, I asked, "Are the Criswells in school, ma'am?"

"Speak up, boy! Who?"

I shouted, "The Criswells!"

Those girls giggled again.

"The Criswells attend the school. And you will have Miss Margaret as your teacher, seeing as you're likely behind."

I ignored her comment and said, "Yes, ma'am," and by then I was grinning, too. I'd see Charles at school. And Margaret would be my teacher.

Darkness set in, and lanterns were lit.

"You're in the attic," said Mrs., handing me one of the lanterns. "You come on down here when you're called."

"Yes, ma'am," I said, and all six girls kept up that group

giggle. The smallest had snuck up beside me and took hold of my hand, pulling me to a set of narrow stairs. I stepped up, but that little hand wouldn't let go.

"Hannah!" barked Mrs.

Hannah let go and clapped her hands together like her own private handshake.

Mrs. said, "Get goin', Jake. And you girls finish your work."

I continued on up, listening to six girls shuffling around, doing whatever work that girls do. At the top of the steps, I seen a ladder. I held on to my lantern tight and climbed on up. Stepping through a opening, I felt dust flying around my face, but it didn't matter. There set my old canvas bag in a attic room way bigger than my cage ever was. I could stretch on out, even run a few steps if I wanted. I knew Mrs. wouldn't like that, so I set down on a old lumpy straw mattress and took off my boots. Nasty smells from inside and outside them boots. I walked them across the room to a six-side window hole filled with a six-side piece of wood. Thought I'd open up that window and air out them boots.

I set the lantern down and tried to get hold of that piece of wood. Pull in, I knew. Wouldn't do to push out and have to run down to pick it up, hoping it didn't crush nobody on the way down. But I couldn't get a grip. It held tight like it grew there. I had to loose it up somehow. A nail laying in the corner caught the lantern light. I picked it up and poked it in all around the six sides.

And then, feet firm against the wall, I grabbed that cover and give the biggest heave I had in me. I ended up on my back with that piece of wood on my chest.

"You better not be breakin' things!" Mrs.'s voice come chasing up the ladder.

"No, ma'am," I hollered. "Just openin' the window."

"You make sure to close it before you leave that attic!" she called out. "And shut off that lantern before you burn the place down."

"Yes, ma'am."

I laid aside the window cover and shut off the lantern. And then I walked to the six-side window opening. Even with a spring chill in the air, I didn't leave that spot all night.

The moon was way brighter than any lantern could ever be. It lit up the valley that run off for miles from that high-up room in that high-up house. And the stars helped out, too, shining and twinkling. And I seen lights in the valley, maybe some of them new electric lights, maybe a street lamp or maybe a house with people settling in for the night.

I took Pa's letter from inside my shirt and tore it into tiny pieces. And then I tossed them one at a time out the window and watched the night breeze take them away.

Here I was in my new life. Full up with hard work and chickens and a hundred dumb sheep. But dinner every day and Charles and Margaret and music and even reading.

And a whole mess of sisters.

Cells at the Old Idaho Penitentiary

AUTHOR'S NOTE

On a scorching hot day in June of 2007, I took a tour of the Old Idaho Penitentiary in Boise, Idaho, a historical site known as the Old Pen. As I tried to find even a sliver of shade, the docent mentioned that the youngest prisoner ever incarcerated there was ten years old. That prisoner's name was James Oscar Baker, and he had served time for manslaughter back in the 1880s.

I couldn't imagine anyone living at that place at that time in history, let alone a ten-year-old kid. No air conditioning. No refrigerators. No electricity at all. And what about winter? Living in a cell without heat. How had he possibly survived?

I contacted the Idaho Historical Society to see what I could find out. They sent me a copy of James's entry from the Convict Registry: James Oscar Baker. Prisoner 88. Received on May 31, 1885. 4'6" tall. Age 10. Sentenced to five years for manslaughter. But there weren't any records of his day-to-day life inside the walls of the Old Pen. That's when Jake's story was born.

Prisoner 88 is not about James Oscar Baker, but Jake's story was inspired by what I learned about James's predicament, including this article that appeared on May 2, 1885, in the *Idaho Register*, a newspaper in Eagle Rock, Idaho:

SHOOTING AT SODA.

E. T. Williams Shot by a Ten Year Old Boy.

We got meager particulars of a shooting scrape which occurred at Soda Springs on Tuesday afternoon. It seems that E. T. Williams, proprietor of the large new hotel there and a man named Campbell, a relative, had been drinking, and entered Mr. Whittier's saloon, which was in charge of J. W. Baker, and called for a pint of whiskey, which Baker told him he could not have unless he produced an order from Mr. Whittier. Williams said they would fool with him until he killed some one, and after repeated requests for the whiskey, and stating that Mr. Whittier said he could have it; accusing Baker of calling him a liar, and after parleying started after Baker, who went around the billiard tables, with Williams after him. After making two or three circuts Campbell stepped up and they then came together. Just at this time a ten year old boy of Baker's who was behind the bar, stepped out with a pistol in hand, and aiming at Williams, shot him through the heart. Baker at once gave himself up as the responsible person, and was taken to Blackfoot where [he] waived examination and was remanded to jail.

According to the trial transcripts from May of 1885, James's case was tried before a jury. The judge explained to the jury, "If the evidence clearly shows that this defendant knows the distinction between good and evil [at the time of the crime], then he is responsible for his acts although he may not be fourteen years of age." Back then, the courts presumed that anyone age fourteen and over automatically knew right from wrong.

Before a verdict was reached, James pleaded guilty to manslaughter, possibly to avoid a harsher sentence if convicted of murder. That was an unfortunate decision. In the Petition for Pardon submitted less than a year later, it was explained that not all of the jury members were convinced that James knew he was doing wrong when he picked up the gun and fired. According to retired Idaho judge Ron Wilper, who interpreted the legal documents for me in May of 2008, because the jury members couldn't reach a unanimous decision, James would have been acquitted.

Instead, James was sentenced to five years. Back then, there weren't any separate facilities for juvenile offenders, so he had to serve his time at the penitentiary. His fellow prisoners were serving time for counterfeiting, assault with a deadly weapon, perjury, first-degree murder, robbery, embezzlement, introducing liquor into Indian country, and even stealing letters from the US mail. Some were miners, ranchers, laborers, or herders. Inmates included Mormon "cohabs" and also Chinese men, who had likely been brought to the United States to build the railroads.

The Old Pen as I depict it in *Prisoner 88* is based on its real history. It was completely self-sufficient from the time it began in 1872 up through the Depression. Prisoners worked on nearby farms and orchards; they did laundry and tended animals. Eventually there was a library and a pig farm. Prisoners actually used dynamite to blast rocks that became the walls of the Old Pen. And, in the 1960s, there really was a prison cat. The Old Pen was closed in 1973.

* * *

After Jake's story was finished, I discovered more information about the boy who inspired *Prisoner 88*. Although I chose to make Jake an only child with only one parent, I knew that James Oscar Baker actually had a mother and father. I was astounded, however, to find that he was one of thirteen siblings! James's parents gave up guardianship of him when he was released from prison, but he eventually reunited with his mother and some of his siblings.

According to census records, James learned to read and write but only attended school for four years. Records also reveal that he worked as a laborer and fought in World War I. He died in 1944.

I hope that he had a good life.

Find the Discussion Guide here: http://bit.ly/Pris88